S0-BQI-906

THE INDIAN LILY

THE INDIAN LILY

AND OTHER STORIES

BY

HERMANN SUDERMANN

TRANSLATED BY

LUDWIG LEWISOHN

Short Story Index Reprint Series

 BOOKS FOR LIBRARIES PRESS
FREEPORT, NEW YORK

First Published 1911
Reprinted 1970

INTERNATIONAL STANDARD BOOK NUMBER:
0-8369-3712-0

LIBRARY OF CONGRESS CATALOG CARD NUMBER:
71-134982

PRINTED IN THE UNITED STATES OF AMERICA

CONTENTS

THE INDIAN LILY

THE INDIAN LILY

I.

It was seven o'clock in the morning when Herr von Niebeldingk opened the iron gate and stepped into the front garden whose wall of blossoming bushes separated the house from the street.

The sun of a May morning tinted the greyish walls with gold, and caused the open window-panes to flash with flame.

The master directed a brief glance at the second story whence floated the dull sound of the carpet-beater. He thrust the key rapidly into the key-hole for a desire stirred in him to slip past the porter's lodge unobserved.

"I seem almost to be—ashamed!" he murmured with a smile of self-derision as a similar impulse overcame him in front of the house door.

But John, his man—a dignified person of fifty—had observed his approach and stood in

9

the opening door. The servant's mutton-chop whiskers and admirably silvered front-lock contrasted with a repressed reproach that hovered between his brows. He bowed deeply.

"I was delayed," said Herr von Niebeldingk, in order to say something and was vexed because this sentence sounded almost like an excuse.

"Do you desire to go to bed, captain, or would you prefer a bath?"

"A bath," the master responded. "I have slept elsewhere."

That sounded almost like another excuse.

"I'm obviously out of practice," he reflected as he entered the breakfast-room where the silver samovar steamed among the dishes of old Sèvres.

He stepped in front of the mirror and regarded himself—not with the forbearance of a friend but the keen scrutiny of a critic.

"Yellow, yellow. . . ." He shook his head. "I must apply a curb to my feelings."

Upon the whole, however, he had reason to be fairly satisfied with himself. His figure, despite the approach of his fortieth year, had remained slender and elastic. The sternly chiselled face, surrounded by a short, half-pointed beard, showed neither flabbiness nor bloat. It was only around the dark, weary eyes that the experiences of the past night had laid a net-work of wrinkles

and shadows.   Ten years ago pleasure had driven
the hair from his temples, but it grew energeti-
cally upon his crown and rose, above his forehead, in a Mephistophelian curve.

The civilian's costume which often lends retired officers a guise of excessive spick-and-span-
ness had gradually combined with an easier bearing to give his figure a natural elegance.   To be
sure, six years had passed since, displeased by a
nagging major, he had definitely hung up the
dragoon's coat of blue.

He was wealthy enough to have been able to
indulge in the luxury of that displeasure.   In
addition his estates demanded more rigorous
management. . . . From Christmas to late
spring he lived in Berlin, where his older brother
occupied one of those positions at court that
mean little enough either to superior or inferior
ranks, but which, in a certain social set depen-
dent upon the court, have an influence of ines-
timable value.   Without assuming the part of
either a social lion or a patron, he used this influence with sufficient thoroughness to be popular, even, in certain cases, to be feared, and belonged to that class of men to whom one always
confides one's difficulties, never one's wife.

John came to announce to his master that the
bath was ready.   And while Niebeldingk
stretched himself lazily in the tepid water he let

his reflections glide serenely about the delightful occurrence of the past night.

That occurrence had been due for six months, but opportunity had been lacking. "I am close-ly watched and well-known," she had told him, "and dare not go on secret errands." . . . Now at last their chance had come and had been used with clever circumspectness. . . . Somewhere on the Polish boundary lived one of her cousins to whose wedding she was permitted to travel alone. . . . She had planned to arrive in Berlin unannounced and, instead of taking the morning train from Eydtkuhnen, to take the train of the previous evening. Thus a night was gained whose history had no necessary place in any family chronicle and the memories of which could, if need were, be obliterated from one's own consciousness. . . . Her arrival and de-parture had caused a few moments of really needless anxiety. That was all. No acquaint-ance had run into them, no waiter had intimated any suspicion, the very cabby who drove them through the dawn had preserved his stupid lack of expression when Niebeldingk suddenly sprang from the vehicle and permitted the lady to be driven on alone. . . .

Before his eyes stood her picture—as he had seen her lying during the night in his arms, fevered with anxiety and rapture . . . Ordinarily her eyes were large and serene, almost drowsy. . . . The night had proven to him what a glow could be kindled in them. Whether her broad brows, growing together over the nose, could be regarded as a beautiful feature—that was an open question. He liked them—so much was certain.

"Thank heaven," he thought. "At last, once more—a *woman*."

And he thought of another who for three years had been allied to him by bonds of the tenderest intimacy and whom he had this night betrayed.

"Between us," he consoled himself, "things will remain as they have been, and I can enjoy my liberty."

He sprayed his body with the icy water of the douche and rang for John who stood outside of the door with a bath-robe.

When, ten minutes later, shivering comfortably, he entered the breakfast-room, he found beside his cup a little heap of letters which the morning post had brought. There were two letters that gripped his attention.

One read:

"Berlin N., Philippstrasse 10 a.
Dear Herr von Niebeldingk:—

For the past week I have been in Berlin studying agriculture, since, as you know, I am to take charge of the estate. Papa made me promise

faithfully to look you up immediately after my
arrival. It is merely due to the respect I owe
you that I haven't kept my promise. As I know
that you won't tell Papa I might as well confess
to you that I've scarcely been sober the whole
week.— Oh, Berlin is a deuce of a place!

If you don't object I will drop in at noon to-
morrow and convey Papa's greetings to you.
Papa is again afflicted with the gout.

With warm regards,
                Your very faithful
                    FRITZ VON EHRENBERG."

The other letter was from . . . her—
clear, serene, full of such literary reminiscences
as always dwelt in her busy little head.

"DEAR FRIEND:—

I wouldn't ask you: Why do I not see you?
—you have not called for five days—I would
wait quietly till your steps led you hither without
persuasion or compulsion; but 'every animal
loves itself' as the old gossip Cicero says, and I
feel a desire to chat with you.

I have never believed, to be sure, that we would
remain indispensable to each other. '*Racine
passera comme le café,*' Mme. de Sévigné says
somewhere, but I would never have dreamed that
we would see so little of each other before the
inevitable end of all things.

You know the proverb: even old iron hates to
rust, and I'm only twenty-five.

Come once again, dear Master, if you care

to. I have an excellent cigarette for you—Blum Pasha. I smoke a little myself now and then, but *c'est plus fort que moi* and ends in head-ache.

Joko has at last learned to say 'Richard.' He trills the *r* cunningly. He knows that he has little need to be jealous.

Good-bye!

ALICE."

He laughed and brought forth her picture which stood, framed and glazed, upon his desk. A delicate, slender figure—"*blonde comme les blés*"—with bluish grey, eager eyes and a mocking expression of the lips—it was she herself, she who had made the last years of his life truly livable and whose fate he administered rather than ruled.

She was the wife of a wealthy mine-owner whose estates abutted on his and with whom an old friendship, founded on common sports, connected him.

One day, suspecting nothing, Niebeldingk entered the man's house and found him dragging his young wife from room to room by the hair. . . . Niebeldingk interfered and felt, in return, the lash of a whip. . . . Time and place had been decided upon when the man's physician forbade the duel. . . . He had been long suspected, but no certain symptoms had been alleged, since the brave little woman revealed nothing of the frightful inwardness of her married life. . . . Three days later he was definitely sent to a sanitarium. But between Niebeldingk and Alice the memory of that last hour of suffering soon wove a thousand threads of helplessness and pity into the web of love.

As she had long lost her parents and as she was quite defenceless against her husband's hostile guardians, the care of her interests devolved naturally upon him. . . . He released her from troublesome obligations and directed her demands toward a safe goal. . . . Then, very tenderly, he lifted her with all the roots of her being from the old, poverty-stricken soil of her earlier years and transplanted her to Berlin where, by the help of his brother's wife—still gently pressing on and smoothing the way himself—he created a new way of life for her.

In a villa, hidden by foliage from Lake Constance, her husband slowly drowsed toward dissolution. She herself ripened in the sharp air of the capital and grew almost into another woman in this banal, disillusioned world, sober even in its intoxication.

Of society, from whose official section her fate as well as her commoner's name separated her, she saw just enough to feel the influence of the essential conceptions that governed it.

She lost diffidence and awkwardness, she became a woman of the world and a connoisseur of life. She learned to condemn one day what she forgave the next, she learned to laugh over nothing and to grieve over nothing and to be indignant over nothing.

But what surprised Niebeldingk more than these small adaptations to the omnipotent spirit of her new environment, was the deep revolution experienced by her innermost being.

She had been a clinging, self-effacing, timid soul. Within three years she became a determined and calculating little person who lacked nothing but a certain fixedness to be a complete character.

A strange coldness of the heart now emanated from her and this was strengthened by precipitate and often unkindly judgment, supported in its turn by a desire to catch her own reflection in all things and to adopt witty points of view.

Nor was this all. She acquired a desire to learn, which at first stimulated and amused Niebeldingk, but which had long grown to be something of a nuisance.

He himself was held, and rightly held, to be a man of intellect, less by virtue of rapid perception and flexible thought, than by virtue of a coolly observant vision of the world, incapable of being confused—a certain healthy cynicism which, though it never lost an element of good

nature, might yet abash and even chill the souls
of men.

His actual knowledge, however, had remained
mere wretched patchwork, his logic came to an
end wherever bold reliance upon the intuitive
process was needed to supply missing links in
the ratiocinative chain.

And so it came to pass that Alice, whom at
first he had regarded as his scholar, his handi-
work, his creature, had developed annoyingly beyond him. . . . Involuntarily and innocently she delivered the keenest thrusts. He had, actually, to be on guard. . . . In the irrespon-
sible delight of intellectual crudity she solved the
deepest problems of humanity; she repeated, full
of faith, the judgments of the ephemeral rapid
writer, instead of venturing upon the sources of
knowledge. Yet even so she impressed him by
her faculty of adaptation and her shining zeal.
He was often silenced, for his slow moving mind
could not follow the vagaries of that rapid little
brain.

What would she be at again to-day? "The old
gossip Cicero. . . ." And, "Mme. de Sévigné remarks. . . ." What a rattling and
tinkling. It provoked him.

And her love! . . . That was a bad business. What is one to do with a mistress who,
before falling asleep, is capable of lecturing on

Schopenhauer's metaphysics of sex, and will prove to you up to the hilt how unworthy it really is to permit oneself to be duped by nature if one does not share her aim for the generations to come?

The man is still to be born upon whom such wisdom, uttered at such an hour—by lips however sweet—does not cast a chill.

Since that philosophical night he had left untouched the little key that hung yonder over his desk and that give him, in her house, the sacred privileges of a husband. And so his life became once more a hunt after new women who filled his heart with unrest and with the foolish fires of youth.

But Alice had never been angry at him. Apparently she lacked nothing. . . .

And his thoughts wandered from her to the woman who had lain against his breast to-night, shuddering in her stolen joy.

Heavens! He had almost forgotten one thing!

He summoned John and said:

"Go to the florist and order a bunch of Indian lilies. The man knows what I mean. If he hasn't any, let him procure some by noon."

John did not move a muscle, but heaven only knew whether he did not suspect the connection between the Indian lilies and the romance of the

past night. It was in his power to adduce prece-
dents.

It was an old custom of Niebeldingk's—a remnant of his half out-lived Don Juan years—to
send a bunch of Indian lilies to those women who
had granted him their supreme favours. He always sent the flowers next morning. Their sym-
bolism was plain and delicate: In spite of what
has taken place you are as lofty and as sacred in
my eyes as these pallid, alien flowers whose home
is beside the Ganges. Therefore have the kind-
ness—not to annoy me with remorse.

It was a delicate action and—a cynical one.

II.

At noon—Niebeldingk had just returned from his morning canter—the visitor, previously announced, was ushered in.

He was a robust young fellow, long of limb and broad of shoulder. His face was round and tanned, with hot, dark eyes. With merry boldness, yet not without diffidence, he sidled, in his blue cheviot suit, into the room.

"Morning, Herr von Niebeldingk."

Enviously and admiringly Niebeldingk surveyed the athletic figure which moved with springy grace.

"Morning, my boy . . . sober?"

"In honour of the day, yes."

"Shall we breakfast?"

"Oh, with delight, Herr von Niebeldingk!"

They passed into the breakfast-room where two covers had already been laid, and while John served the caviare the flood of news burst which had mounted in their Franconian home during the past months.

Three betrothals, two important transfers of land, a wedding, Papa's gout, Mama's charities, Jenny's new target, Grete's flirtation with the

American engineer. And, above all things, the examination!

"Dear Herr von Niebeldingk, it's a rotten farce. For nine years the gymnasium trains you and drills you, and in the end you don't get your trouble's worth! I'm sorry for every hour of cramming I did. They released me from the oral exam., simply sent me out like a monkey when I was just beginning to let my light shine! Did you ever hear of such a thing? *Did* you ever?"

"Well, and how about your university work, Fritz?"

That was a ticklish business, the youth averred. Law and political science was no use. Every ass took that up. And since it was after all only his purpose to pass a few years of his green youth profitably, why he thought he'd stick to his trade and find out how to plant cabbages properly.

"Have you started in anywhere yet?"

Oh, there was time enough. But he had been to some lectures—agronomy and inorganic chemistry. . . . You have to begin with inorganic chemistry if you want to go in for organic. And the latter was agricultural chemistry which was what concerned him.

He made these instructive remarks with a serious air and poured down glass after glass of Madeira. His cheeks began to glow, his heart expanded.

"But that's all piffle, Herr von Niebeldingk,
. . . all this bookworm business can go to
the devil . . . Life—life—life—that's the
main thing!"

"What do you call life, Fritz?"

With both hands he stroked the velvety surface
of his close-cropped skull.

"Well, how am I to tell you? D'you know how
I feel? As if I were standing in front of a great,
closed garden . . . and I know that all
Paradise is inside . . . and occasionally a
strain of music floats out . . . and occasionally a white garment glitters . . . and
I'd like to get in and I can't. That's life, you
see. And I've got to stand miserably outside?"

"Well, you don't impress me as such a miserable creature?"

"No, no, in a way, not. On the coarser side, so
to speak, I have a good deal of fun. Out there
around *Philippstrasse* and *Marienstrasse* there
are women enough—stylish and fine-looking and
everything you want. And my friends are great
fellows, too. Every one can stand his fifteen
glasses . . . I suppose I am an ass . . .
and perhaps it's only moral *katzenjammer* on
account of this past week. But when I walk the
streets and see the tall, distinguished houses and
think of all those people and their lives, yonder
a millionaire, here a minister of state, and think

that, once upon a time, they were all crude boys like myself—well, then I have the feeling as if I'd never attain anything, but always remain what I am."

"Well, my dear Fritz, the only remedy for that lies in that 'book-worm business' as you call it. Sit down on your breeches and work!"

"No, Herr von Niebeldingk, it isn't that either . . . let me tell you. Day before yesterday I was at the opera . . . They sang the *Götterdämmerung*. . . . You know, of course. There is *Siegfried*, a fellow like myself. . . . not more than twenty . . . I sat upstairs in the third row with two seam-stresses. I'd picked them up in the *Chaussee-strasse*—cute little beasts, too. . . . But when *Brunhilde* stretched out her wonderful, white arms to him and sang: 'On to new deeds, O hero!' why I felt like taking the two girls by the scruff of the neck and pitching them down into the pit. I was so ashamed. Because, you see, *Siegfried* had his *Brunhilde* who inspired him to do great deeds. And what have I? . . . A couple of hard cases picked up in the street."

"Afterwards, I suppose, you felt more recon-ciled?"

"That shows how little you know me. I'd promised the girls supper. So I had to eat with them. But when that was over I let 'em slide. I ran about in the streets and just—howled!"

"Very well, but what exactly are you after?"

"That's what I don't know, Herr von Niebeldingk. Oh, if I knew! But it's something quite indefinite—hard to think, hard to comprehend. I'd like to howl with laughter and I don't know why . . . to shriek, and I don't know what about."

"Blessed youth!" Niebeldingk thought, and looked at the enthusiastic boy full of emotion.

. . .

John, who was serving, announced that the florist's girl had come with the Indian lilies.

"Indian lilies, what sort of lilies are they?" asked Fritz overcome by a hesitant admiration.

"You'll see," Niebeldingk answered and ordered the girl to be admitted.

She struggled through the door, a half-grown thing with plump red cheeks and smooth yellow hair. Diffident and frightened, she nevertheless began to flirt with Fritz. In front of her she held the long stems of the exotic lilies whose blossoms, like gigantic narcissi, brooded in star-like rest over chaste and alien dreams. From the middle of each chalice came a sharp, green shimmer which faded gently along the petals of the flowers.

"Confound it, but they're beautiful!" cried

Fritz. "Surely they have quite a peculiar significance."

Niebeldingk arose, wrote the address without permitting John, who stood in suspicious proximity, to throw a glance at it, handed cards and flowers to the girl, gave her a tip, and escorted her to the door himself.

"So they do mean something special?" Fritz asked eagerly. He couldn't get over his enthusiasm.

"Yes, my boy."

"And may one know. . . . "

"Surely, one may know. I give these lilies to that lady whose lofty purity transcends all doubt —I give them as a symbol of my chaste and desireless admiration."

Fritz's eyes shone.

"Ah, but I'd like to know a lady like that— some day!" he cried and pressed his hands to his forehead.

"That will come! That will come!" Niebeldingk tapped the youth's shoulder calmingly. "Will you have some salad?"

III.

Around the hour of afternoon tea Niebeldingk, true to a dear, old habit, went to see his friend.

She inhabited a small second-floor apartment in the *Regentenstrasse* which he had himself selected for her when she came as a stranger to Berlin. With flowers and palms and oriental rugs she had moulded a delicious retreat, and before her bed-room windows the nightingales sang in the springtime.

She seemed to be expecting him. In the great, raised bay, separated from the rest of the drawing-room by a thicket of dark leaves, the stout tea-urn was already expectantly humming.

In a bright, girlish dress, devoid of coquetry or pouting, Alice came to meet him.

"I'm glad you're here again, Richard."

That was all.

He wanted to launch out into the tale which he had meant to tell her, but she cut him short.

"Since when do I demand excuses, Richard? You come and there you are. And if you don't come, I have to be content too."

27

"You should really be a little less tolerant," he warned her.

"A blessed lot it would help me," she answered merrily.

Gently she took his arm and led him to his old place. Then silently, and with that restrained eagerness that characterised all her actions she busied herself with the tea-urn.

His critical and discriminating gaze followed her movements. With swift, delicate gestures she pushed forward the Chinese dish, shook the tea from the canister and poured the first drops of boiling water through a sieve. . . . Her quick, bird-like head moved hither and thither, and the bow of the orange-coloured ribbon which surrounded her over-delicate neck trembled a little with every motion.

"She really is the most charming of all," such was the end of his reflections, "if only she weren't so damnably sensible."

Silently she took her seat opposite him, folded her white hands in her lap, and looked into his eyes with such significant archness that he began to feel embarrassed.

Had she any suspicion of his infidelities?

Surely not. No jealous woman can look about her so calmly and serenely.

"What have you been doing all this time?" he asked.

"I? Good heavens! Look about you and you'll see."

She pointed to a heap of books which lay scattered over the window seat and sewing table.

There were Moltke's letters and the memoirs of von Schön, and Max Müller's Aryan studies. Nor was the inevitable Schopenhauer lacking.

"What are you after with all that learning?" he asked.

"Ah, dear friend, what is one to do? One can't always be going about in strange houses. Do you expect me to stand at the window and watch the clouds float over the old city-wall?"

He had the uncomfortable impression that she was quoting something again.

"My mood," she went on, "is in what Goethe calls the minor of the soul. It is the yearning that reaches out afar and yet restrains itself harmoniously within itself. Isn't that beautifully put?"

"It may be, but it's too high for me!" In laughing self-protection, he stretched out his arms toward her.

"Don't make fun of me," she said, slightly shamed, and arose.

"And what is the object of your yearning?" he asked in order to leave the realm of Goethe as swiftly as possible.

"Not you, you horrible person," she answered and, for a moment, touched his hair with her lips.

"I know that, dearest," he said, "it's a long time since you've sent me two notes a day."

"And since you came to see me twice daily," she returned and gazed at the floor with a sad irony.

"We have both changed greatly, Alice."

"We have indeed, Richard."

A silence ensued.

His eyes wandered to the opposite wall. . . . His own picture, framed in silvery maple-wood, hung there. . . . Behind the frame appeared a bunch of blossoms, long faded and shrivelled to a brownish, indistinguishable heap.

These two alone knew the significance of the flowers. . . .

"Were you at least happy in those days, Alice?"

"You know I am always happy, Richard."

"Oh yes, yes; I know your philosophy. But I meant happy with me, through me?"

She stroked her delicate nose thoughtfully. The mocking expression about the corners of her mouth became accentuated.

"I hardly think so, Richard," she said after an interval. "I was too much afraid of you . . . I seemed so stupid in comparison to you and I feared that you would despise me."

"That fear, at least, you have overcome very thoroughly?" he asked.

"Not wholly, Richard. Things have only shifted their basis. Just as, in those days, I felt ashamed of my ignorance, so now I feel ashamed —no, that isn't the right word. . . . But all this stuff that I store up in my head seems to weigh upon me in my relations with you. I seem to be a nuisance with it. . . . You men, especially mature men like yourself, seem to know all these things better, even when you don't know them. . . . The precise form in which a given thought is presented to us may be new to you, but the thought itself you have long digested. It's for this reason that I feel intimidated whenever I approach you with my pursuits. 'You might better have held your peace,' I say to myself. But what am I to do? I'm so profoundly interested!"

"So you really need the society of a rather stupid fellow, one to whom all this is new and who will furnish a grateful audience?"

"Stupid? No," she answered, "but he ought to be inexperienced. He ought himself to want to learn things. . . . He ought not to assume a compassionate expression as who should say: 'Ah, my dear child, if you knew what I know, and how indifferent all those things are to me!' . . . For these things are not indifferent, Richard, not

to me, at least. . . .   And for the sake of the
joy I take in them, you . . ."

"Strange how she sees through me," he reflected. "I wonder she clings to me as she does."

And while he was trying to think of something
that might help her, the dear boy came into his
mind who had to-day divulged to him the sorrows
of youth and whom the unconscious desire for a
higher plane of life had driven weeping through
the streets.

"I know of some one for you."

Her expression was serious.

"You know of some one for me," she repeated
with painful deliberateness.

"Don't misunderstand me. It's a playfellow,
a pupil—something in the nature of a pastime,
anything you will."

He told her the story of *Siegfried* and the two
seamstresses.

She laughed heartily.

"I was afraid you wanted to be rid of me,"
she said, laying her forehead for a few moments
against his sleeve.

"Shame on you," he said, carelessly stroking
her hair. "But what do you think? Shall I
bring the young fellow?"

"You may very well bring him," she answered.
There was a look of pain about her mouth.
"Doesn't one even train young poodles?"

IV.

THREE days later, at the same hour of the afternoon, the student, Fritz von Ehrenberg entered Niebeldingk's study.

"I have summoned you, dear friend, because I want to introduce you to a charming young woman," Niebeldingk said, arising from his desk.

"Now?" Fritz asked, sharply taken aback.

"Why not?"

"Why, I'd have to get my—my afternoon coat first and fix myself up a bit. What is the lady to think of me?"

"I'll take care of that. Furthermore, you probably know her, at least by reputation."

He mentioned the name of her husband which was known far and wide in their native province,

Fritz knew the whole story.

"Poor lady!" he said. "Papa and Mama have often felt sorry for her. I suppose her husband is still living."

Niebeldingk nodded.

"People all said that you were going to marry her."

"Is *that* what people said?"

"Yes, and Papa thought it would be a piece of great good fortune."

"For whom?"

"I beg your pardon, I suppose that was tactless, Herr von Niebeldingk."

"It was, dear Fritz.—But don't worry about it, just come."

The introduction went smoothly. Fritz behaved as became the son of a good family, was respectful but not stiff, and answered her friendly questions briefly and to the point.

"He's no discredit to me," Niebeldingk thought.

As for Alice, she treated her young guest with a smiling, motherly care which was new in her and which filled Niebeldingk with quiet pleasure. . . . On other occasions she had assumed toward young men a tone of wise, faint interest which meant clearly: "I will exhaust your possibilities and then drop you." To-day she showed a genuine sympathy which, though its purpose may have been to test him the more sharply, seemed yet to bear witness to the pure and free humanity of her soul.

She asked him after his parental home and was charmed with his naïve rapture at escaping the psychical atmosphere of the cradle-songs of his mother's house. She was also pleased with his attitude toward his younger brothers and sisters, equally devoid, as it was, of exaggeration or condescension. Everything about him seemed to her simple and sane and full of ardour after information and maturity.

Niebeldingk sat quietly in his corner ready, at need, to smooth over any outbreak of uncouth youthfulness. But there was no occasion. Fritz confined himself within the limits of modest liberty and used his mind vigorously but with devout respect and delighted obedience. Once only, when the question of the necessity of authority came up, did he go far.

"I don't give a hang for any authority," he said. "Even the mild compulsion of what are called high-bred manners may go to the deuce for me!"

Niebeldingk was about to interfere with some reconciling remark when he observed, to his astonishment, that Alice who, as a rule, was bitterly hostile to all strident unconventionality, had taken no offence.

"Let him be, Niebeldingk," she said. "As far as he is concerned he is, doubtless, in the right. And nothing would be more shameful than if society were already to begin to make a featureless model boy of him."

"That will never be, I swear to you, dear lady," cried Fritz all aglow and stretching out his hands to ward off imaginary chains.

Niebeldingk smiled and thought: "So much the better for him." Then he lit a fresh cigarette.

The conversation turned to learned things. Fritz, paraphrasing Tacitus, vented his hatred of the Latin civilisations. Alice agreed with him and quoted Mme. de Staël. Niebeldingk arose, quietly meeting the reproachful glance of his beloved.

Fritz jumped up simultaneously, but Niebeldingk laughingly pushed him back into his seat.

"You just stay," he said, "our dear friend is only too eager to slaughter a few more peoples."

V.

WHEN he dropped in at Alice's a few days later he found her sitting, hot-cheeked and absorbed, over Strauss's *Life of Jesus*.

"Just fancy," she said, holding up her forehead for his kiss, "that young poodle of yours is making me take notice. He gives me intellectual nuts to crack. It's strange how this young generation——"

"I beg of you, Alice," he interrupted her, "you are only a very few years his senior."

"That may be so," she answered, "but the little education I have derives from another epoch. . . . I am, metaphysically, as unexacting as the people of your generation. A certain fogless freedom of thought seemed to me until to-day the highest point of human development."

"And Fritz von Ehrenberg, student of agriculture, has converted you to a kind of thoughtful religiosity?" he asked, smiling good-naturedly.

In her zeal she wasn't even aware of his irony.

"We're not going to give in so easily. . . . But it is strange what an impression is made on one by a current of strong and natural feeling. . . . This young fellow comes to me and says:

'There is a God, for I feel Him and I need Him. Prove the contrary if you can.' . . . Well, so I set about proving the contrary to him. But our poor negations have become so glib that one has forgotten the reasons for them. Finally he defeated me along the whole line . . . so I sat down at once and began to study up . . . just as one would polish rusty weapons . . . Bible criticism and DuBois-Reymond and 'Force and Matter' and all the things that are tradition- ally irrefutable.''

"And that amuses you?" he asked compassion- ately.

A theoretical indignation took hold of her that always amused him greatly.

"Does it amuse me? Are such things proper subjects for amusement? Surely you must use other expressions, Richard, when one is concerned for the most sacred goods of humanity. . . ."

"Forgive me," he said, "I didn't mean to touch those things irreverently."

She stroked his arm softly, thus dumbly ask- ing forgiveness in her turn.

"But now," she continued, "I am equipped once more, and when he comes to-morrow——"

"So he's coming to-morrow?"

"Naturally, . . . then you will see how I'll send him home sorely whipped . . . I can defeat him with Kant's antinomies alone.

. . . And when it comes to what people call 'revelation,' well! . . . But I assure you, my dear one, I'm not very happy defending this icy, nagging criticism. . . . To be quite sincere, I would far rather be on his side. Warmth is there and feeling and something positive to support one. Would you like some tea?"

"Thanks, no, but some brandy."

Rapidly brushing the waves of hair from her drawn forehead she ran into the next room and returned with the bottle bearing three stars on its label from which she herself took a tiny drop occasionally—"when my mind loses tone for study" as she was wont to say in self-justification.

A crimson afterglow, reflected from the walls of the houses opposite, filled the little drawing-room in which the mass of feminine ornaments glimmered and glittered.

"I've really become quite a stranger here," he thought, regarding all these things with the curiosity of one who has come after an absence. From each object hung, like a dewdrop, the memory of some exquisite hour.

"You look about you so," Alice said with an undertone of anxiety in her voice, "don't you like it here any longer?"

"What are you thinking of," he exclaimed, "I like it better daily."

She was about to reply but fell silent and looked into space with a smile of wistful irony.

"If I except the *Life of Jesus* and the Kantian —what do you call the things?"

"Antinomies."

"Aha—*anti* and *nomos*—I understand—well, if I except these dusty superfluities, I may say that your furnishings are really faultless. The quotations from Goethe are really more appropriate, although I could do without them."

"I'll have them swept out," she said in playful submission.

"You are a dear girl," he said playfully and passed his hand caressingly over her severely combed hair.

She grasped his arm with both hands and remained motionless for a moment during which her eyes fastened themselves upon his with a strangely rigid gleam.

"What evil have I done?" he asked. "Do you remember our childhood's verse: 'I am small, my heart is pure?' Have mercy on me."

"I was only playing at passion," she said with the old half-wistful, half-mocking smile, "in order that our relations may not lose solid ground utterly."

"What do you mean?" he asked, pretending astonishment.

"And do you really think, Richard, that between us, things, being as they are—are right?"

"I can't imagine any change that could take place at present."

She hid a hot flush of shame. She was obviously of the opinion that he had interpreted her meaning in the light of a desire for marriage. All earthly possibilities had been discussed between them: this one alone had been sedulously avoided in all their conversations.

"Don't misunderstand me," he continued, determined to skirt the dangerous subject with grace and ease, "there's no question here of anything external, of any change of front with reference to the world. It's far too late for that. . . . Let us remain—if I may so put it—in our spiritual four walls. Given our characters or, I had better say, given your character I see no other relation between us that promises any permanence. . . . If I were to pursue you with a kind of infatuation, or you me with jealousy—it would be insupportable to us both."

She did not reply but gently rolled and unrolled the narrow, blue silk scarf of her gown.

"As it is, we live happily and at peace," he went on, "Each of us has liberty and an individual existence and yet we know how deeply rooted our hearts are in each other."

She heaved a sigh of painful oppression.

"Aren't you content?" he asked.

"For heaven's sake! Surely!" Her voice was frightened. "No one could be more content than I. If only——"

"Well—what?"

"If only it weren't for the lonely evenings!"

A silence ensued. This was a sore point and had always been. He knew it well. But he had to have his evenings to himself. There was nothing to be done about that.

"You musn't think me immodest in my demands," she went on in hasty exculpation. "I'm not even aiming my remarks at you . . . I'm only thinking aloud. . . . But you see, I can't get any real foothold in society until—until my affairs are more clarified. . . . To run about the drawing-rooms as an example of frivolous heedlessness—that's not my way. . . . I can always hear them whisper behind me: 'She doesn't take it much to heart, that shows . . .' No, I'd rather stay at home. I have no friends either and what chance had I to make them? You were always my one and only friend. . . . My books remain. And that's very well by day . . . but when the lamps are lit I begin to throb and ache and run about . . . and I listen for the trill of the door-bell. But no one comes, nothing—except the evening paper. And that's only in winter. Now it's brought before dusk. And in the end there's nothing worth while in it. . . . And so life goes day after day. At last one creeps into bed at half-past nine and, of course, has a wretched night."

"Well, but how am I to help you, dear child?" he asked thoughtfully. He was touched by her quiet, almost serene complaint. "If we took to passing our evenings together, scandal would soon have us by the throat, and then—woe to you!"

Her eager eyes gazed bravely at him.

"Well," she said at last," suppose——"

"What?"

"Never mind. I don't want you to think me unwomanly. And what I've been describing to you is, after all, only a symptom. There's a kind of restlessness in me that I can't explain. . . . If I were of a less active temper, things would be better. . . . It sounds paradoxical, but just because I have so much activity in me, do I weary so quickly. Goethe said once——"

He raised his hands in laughing protest.

She was really frightened.

"Ah, yes, forgive me," she cried. "All that was to be swept out. . . . How forgetful one can be. . . ."

Smiling, she leaned her head against his shoulder and was not to be persuaded from her silence.

VI.

"THERE are delicate boundaries within the realm of the eternal womanly,"—thus Niebeldingk reflected next day,—"in which one is sorely puzzled as to what one had better put into an envelope: a poem or a cheque."

His latest adventure—the cause of these reflections—had blossomed, the evening before, like the traditional rose on the dungheap.

One of his friends who had travelled about the world a good deal and who now assumed the part of the full-blown Parisian, had issued invitations to a house-warming in his new bachelor-apartment. He had invited a number of his gayer friends and ladies exclusively from so-called artistic circles. So far all was quite Parisian. Only the journalists who might, next morning, have proclaimed the glory of the festivity to the world—these were excluded. Berlin, for various reasons, did not seem an appropriate place for that.

It was a rather dreary sham orgy. Even chaperones were present. Several ladies had carefully brought them and they could scarcely be put out. Other ladies even thought it incumbent upon them to ask after the wives of the gentlemen present and to turn up their noses when it appeared that these were conspicuous by their absence. It was upon this occasion, however, that some beneficent chance assigned to Niebeldingk a sighing blonde who remained at his side all evening.

Her name was Meta, she belonged to one of the "best families" of Posen, she lived in Berlin with her mother who kept a boarding house for ladies of the theatre. She herself nursed the ardent desire to dedicate herself to art, for "the ideal" had always been the guiding star of her existence.

At the beginning of supper she expressed herself with a fine indignation concerning the ladies present into whose midst—she assured him eagerly—she had fallen through sheer accident. Later she thawed out, assumed a friendly companionableness to these despised individuals and, in order to raise Niebeldingk's delight to the highest point, admitted with maidenly frankness the indescribable and mysterious attraction toward him which she had felt at the first glance.

Of course, her principles were impregnable. He mustn't doubt that. She would rather seek a moist death in the waves than . . . and so forth.

Although she made this solemn proclamation over the dessert, the consequence of it all was an intimate visit to Niebeldingk's dwelling which came to a bitter sweet end at three o'clock in the morning with gentle tears concerning the wickedness of men in general and of himself in particular. . . .

An attack of *katzenjammer*—such as is scarcely ever spared worldly people of forty—threw a sobering shadow upon this event. The shadow crept forward too, and presaged annoyance.

He was such an old hand now, and didn't even know into what category she really fitted. Was it, after all, impossible that behind all this frivolity the desire to take up the struggle for existence on cleanly terms stuck in her little head?

At all events he determined to spare the possible wounding of outraged womanliness and to wait before putting any final stamp upon the nature of their relations. Hence he set out to play the tender lover by means of the well-tried device of a bunch of Indian lilies.

When he was about to give the order for the flowers to John who always, upon these occasions, assumed a conscientiously stupid expression, a new doubt overcame him.

Was he not desecrating the gift which had brought consolation and absolution to many a remorseful heart, by sending it to a girl who, for all he knew, played a sentimental part only as a matter of decent form? . . . Wasn't there grave danger of her assuming an undue self-importance when she felt that she was taken tragically?

"Well, what did it matter? . . . A few flowers! . . ."

Early on the evening of the next day Meta reappeared. She was dressed in sombre black. She wept persistently and made preparations to stay.

Niebeldingk gave her to understand that, in the first place, he had no more time for her that evening, and that, in the second place, she would do well to go home at a proper hour and spare herself the reproaches of her mother.

"Oh, my little mother, my little mother," she wailed. "How shall I ever present myself to her sight again? Keep me, my beloved! I can never approach my mother again."

He rang for his hat and gloves.

When she saw that he was serious she wept a few more perfunctory tears and went.

Her visits repeated themselves and didn't become any more delightful. On the contrary . . . the heart-broken maiden gave him to understand that her lost honour could be restored only by the means of a speedy marriage.

This exhausted his patience. He saw that he had been thoroughly taken in and so, observing all necessary considerateness, he sent her definitely about her business.

Next day the "little mother" appeared on the scene. She was a dignified woman of fifty, equipped as the Genius of Vengeance, exceedingly glib of tongue and by no means sentimental.

As she belonged to one of the first families of Posen, it was her duty to lay particular stress upon the honour of her daughter whom he had lured to his house and there wickedly seduced. . . . She was prepared to repel any overtures toward a compromise. She belonged to one of the best families of Posen and was not prepared to sell her daughter's virtue. The only possible way of adjusting the matter was an immediate marriage.

Thereupon she began to scream and scold and John, who acted as master of ceremonies, escorted her with a patronising smile to the door. . . .

Next came the visits of an old gentleman in a Prince Albert and the ribbon of some decoration in his button-hole.—John had strict orders to admit no strangers. But the old gentleman was undaunted. He came morning, noon and night and finally settled down on the stairs where Niebeldingk could not avoid meeting him. He was the uncle of Miss Meta, a former servant of the government and a knight of several honourable orders. As such it was his duty to demand the immediate restitution of his niece's honour, else——

Niebeldingk simply turned his back and the knight of several honourable orders trotted, grumbling, down the stairs.

Up to this point Niebeldingk had striven to regard the whole business in a humorous light. It now began to promise serious annoyance. He told the story at his club and the men laughed boisterously, but no one knew anything to the detriment of Miss Meta. She had been introduced by a lady who played small parts at a large theatre and important parts at a small one. The lady was called to account for her protegée. She refused to speak.

"It's all the fault of those accursed Indian lilies," Niebeldingk grumbled one afternoon at his window as he watched the knight of various honourable orders parade the street as undaunted as ever. "Had I treated her with less delicacy, she would never have risked playing the part of an innocent victim."

At that moment John announced Fritz von Ehrenberg.

The boy came in dressed in an admirably fitting summer suit. He was radiant with youth and strength, victory gleamed in his eye; a hymn of victory seemed silently singing on his lips.

"Well Fritz, you seem merry," said Niebeldingk and patted the boy's shoulder. He could not suppress a smile of sad envy.

"Don't ask me! Why shouldn't I be happy? Life is so beautiful, yes, beautiful. Only you musn't have any dealings with women. That plays the deuce with one."

"You don't know yourself how right you are," Niebeldingk sighed, looking out of the corner of an eye at the knight of several honourable orders who had now taken up his station in the shelter of the house opposite.

"Oh, but I do know it," Fritz answered. "If I could describe to you the contempt with which I regard my former mode of life . . . everything is different . . . different . . . so much purer . . . nobler . . . I'm absolutely a stoic now. . . . And that gives one a feeling of such peace, such serenity! And I have you to thank for it, Herr von Niebeldingk."

"I don't understand that. To teach in the *stoa* is a new employment for me."

"Well, didn't you introduce me to that noble lady? Wasn't it you?"

"Aha," said Niebeldingk. The image of

'Alice, smiling a gentle reproach, arose before him.

In the midst of this silly and sordid business that had overtaken him, he had almost lost sight of her. More than a week had passed since he had crossed her threshold.

"How is the dear lady?" he asked.

"Oh, splendid," Fritz said, "just splendid."

"Have you seen her often?"

"Certainly," Fritz replied, "we're reading Marcus Aurelius together now."

"Thank heaven," Niebeldingk laughed, "I see that she's well taken care of."

He made up his mind to see her within the next hour.

Fritz who had only come because he needed to overflow to some one with the joy of life that was in him, soon started to go.

At the door he turned and said timidly and with downcast eyes.

"I have one request to make——"

"Fire away, Fritz! How much?"

"Oh, I don't need money . . . I'd like to have the address of your florist . . . I'd like to send to the dear lady a bunch of the . . . the Indian lilies."

"What? Are you mad?" Niebeldingk cried.

"Why do you ask that?" Fritz was hurt. "May I not also send that symbol to a lady whose purity and loftiness of soul I reverence. I suppose I'm old enough!"

"I see. You're quite right. Forgive me." Niebeldingk bit his lips and gave the lad the address.

Fritz thanked him and went.

Niebeldingk gave way to his mirth and called for his hat. He wanted to go to her at once. But—for better or worse—he changed his mind, for yonder in the gateway, unabashed, stood the knight of several honourable orders.

VII.

To be sure, one can't stand eternally in a gateway. Finally the knight deserted his post and vanished into a sausage shop. The hour had come when even the most glowing passion of revenge fades gently into a passion for supper.

Niebeldingk who had waited behind his curtain, half-amused, half-bored—for in the silent, distinguished street where everyone knew him a scandal was to be avoided at any cost—Niebeldingk hastened to make up for his neglect at once.

The dark fell. Here and there the street-lamps flickered through the purple air of the summer dusk. . . .

The maid who opened the door looked at him with cool astonishment as though he were half a stranger who had the audacity to pay a call at this intimate hour.

"That means a scolding," he thought.

But he was mistaken.

Smiling quietly, Alice arose from the couch where she had been sitting by the light of a shaded lamp and stretched out her hand with all her old kindliness.

The absence of the otherwise inevitable book was the only change that struck him.

"We haven't seen each other for a long time," he said, making a wretched attempt at an explanation.

"Is it so long?" she asked frankly.

"Thank you for your gentle punishment." He kissed her hand. Then he chatted, more or less at random, of disagreeable business matters, of preparations for a journey, and so forth.

"So you are going away?" she asked tensely.

The word had escaped him, he scarcely knew how. Now that he had uttered it, however, he saw very clearly that nothing better remained for him to do than to carry the casual thought into action. . . . Here he passed a fruitless, enervating life, slothful, restless and humiliating; at home there awaited him light, useful work, dreamless sleep, and the tonic sense of being the master.

All that, in other days, held him in Berlin, namely, this modest, clever, flexible woman had almost passed from his life. Steady neglect had done its work. If he went now, scarcely the smallest gap would be torn into the fabric of his life.

Or did it only seem so? Was she more deeply rooted in his heart than he had ever confessed even to himself?

They were both silent. She stood very near him and sought to read the answer to her question in his eyes. A kind of anxious joy appeared upon her slightly worn features.

"I'm needed at home," he said at last. "It is high time for me. If you desire I'll look after your affairs too."

"Mine? Where?"

"Well, I thought we were neighbours there— more than here. Or have you forgotten the estate?"

"Let us leave aside the matter of being neighbours," she answered, "and I don't suppose that I have much voice in the management of the estate as long as—he lives. The guardians will see to that."

"But you could run down there once in a while . . . in the summer for instance. Your place is always ready for you. I saw to that."

"Ah, yes, you saw to that." The wistful irony that he had so often noted was visible again.

For the first time he understood its meaning.

"She has made things too easy for me," he reflected. "I should have felt my chains. Then, too, I would have realised what I possessed in her."

But did he not still possess her? What, after all, had changed since those days of quiet companionship? Why should he think of her as lost to him?

He could not answer this question. But he felt a dull restlessness. A sense of estrangement told him: All is not here as it was.

"Since when do you live in dreams, Alice?" he asked, surveying the empty table by which he had found her.

His question had been innocent, but it seemed to carry a sting. She blushed and looked past him.

"How do you mean?"

"Good heavens, to sit all evening without books and let the light burn in vain—that was not your wont heretofore."

"Oh, that's it. Ah well, one can't be poking in books all the time. And for the past few days my eyes have been aching."

"With secret tears?" he teased.

She gave him a wide, serious look.

"With secret tears," she repeated.

"*Ah perfido!*" he trilled, in order to avoid the scene which he feared. . . . But he was on the wrong scent. She herself interrupted him with the question whether he would stay to supper.

He was curious to find the causes of the changes that he felt here. For that reason and

also because he was not without compunction, he
consented to stay.

She rang and ordered a second cover to be
laid.

Louise looked at her mistress with a disap-
proving glance and went.

"Dear me," he laughed, "the servants are
against me . . . I am lost."

"You have taken to noticing such things very
recently." She gave a perceptible shrug.

"When a wife tells a husband of his newly acquired habits, he is doubly lost," he answered and
gave her his arm.

The silver gleamed on the table . . . the
tea-kettle puffed out delicate clouds . . . exquisitely tinted apples, firm as in Autumn,
smiled at him.

A word of admiration escaped him. And
then, once more, he saw that tragic smile on her
lips—sad, wistful, almost compassionate.

"My darling," he said with sudden tenderness
and caressed her shoulder.

She nodded and smiled. That was all.

At table her mood was an habitual one. Perhaps she was a trifle gentler. He attributed
that to his approaching departure.

She drank a glass of Madeira at the beginning
of the meal, the light Rhine wine she took in

long, thirsty draughts, she even touched the brandy at the meal's end.

An inner fire flared in her. He suspected that, he felt it. She had touched no food. But she permitted nothing to appear on the surface. On the contrary, the emotional warmth that she had shown earlier disappeared. The play of her thoughts grew cooler, clearer, more cutting, the longer she talked.

Twice or thrice quotations from Goethe were about to escape her, but she did not utter them. Smiling she tapped her own lips.

When he observed that she was really restraining a genuine impulse he begged her to consider the protest he had once uttered as merely a jest, perhaps even an ill-considered one. But she said: "Let be, it is as well."

They conversed, as they had often done, of the perished days of their old love. They spoke like two beings who have long conquered all the struggles of the heart and who, in the calm harbour of friendship, regard with equanimity the storms which they have weathered.

This way of speaking had gradually, and with a kind of jocular moroseness, crept into their intercourse. The exciting thing about it was the silent reservation felt by both: We know how different things could be, so soon as we desired.

To-day, for the first time, this game at renunciation seemed to become serious.

"How strange!" he thought. "Here we sit who are dearest to each other in all the world and a kind of futile arrogance drives us farther and farther apart."

Alice arose.

He kissed her, as was his wont, upon hand and forehead and noted how she turned aside with a slight shiver. Then suddenly she took his head in both her hands and kissed him full on the lips with a kind of desperate eagerness.

"Ah," he cried, "what is that? It's more than I have a right to expect."

"Forgive me," she said, withdrawing herself at once. "We're poverty stricken folk and haven't much to give each other."

"After what I have just experienced, I'm inclined to believe the contrary."

But she seemed little inclined to draw the logical consequences of her action. Quietly she gave him his wonted cigarette, lit her own, and sat down in her old place. With rounded lips she blew little clouds of smoke against the table-cover.

"Whenever I regard you in this manner," he said, carefully feeling his way, "it always seems to me that you have some silent reservation, as though you were waiting for something."

"It may be," she answered, blushing anew, "I sit by the way-side, like the man in the story, and think of the coming of my fate."

"Fate? What fate?"

"Ah, who can tell, dear friend? That which one foresees is no longer one's fate!"

"Perhaps it's just the other way."

She drew back sharply and looked past him in tense thoughtfulness. "Perhaps you are right," she said, with a little mysterious sigh. "It may be as you say."

He was no wiser than he had been. But since he held it beneath his dignity to assume the part of the jealous master, he abandoned the search for her secrets with a shrug. The secrets could be of no great importance. No one knew better than himself the moderateness of her desires, no lover, in calm possession of his beloved, had so little to fear as he. . . .

They discussed their plans for the Summer. He intended to go to the North Sea in Autumn, an old affection attracted her to Thuringia. The possibility of their meeting was touched only in so far as courtesy demanded it.

And once more silence fell upon the little drawing-room. Through the twilight an old, phantastic Empire clock announced the hurrying minutes with a hoarse tick.

In other days a magical mood had often filled

this room—the presage of an exquisite flame and its happy death. All that had vibrated here. Nothing remained. They had little to say to each other. That was what time had left.

He played thoughtfully with his cigarette. She stared into nothingness with great, dreamy eyes.

And suddenly she began to weep. . . . He almost doubted his own perception, but the great glittering tears ran softly down her smiling face.

But he was satiated with women's tears. In the fleeting amatory adventures of the past weeks and months, he had seen so many—some genuine, some sham, all superfluous. And so instead of consoling her, he conceived a feeling of sarcasm and nausea: "Now even she carries on!". . . .

The idea did indeed flash into his mind that this moment might be decisive and pregnant with the fate of the future, but his horror of scenes and explanations restrained him.

Wearily he assumed the attitude of one above the storms of the soul and sought a jest with which to recall her to herself. But before he found it she pressed her handkerchief to her eyes and slipped from the room.

"So much the better," he thought and lit a

fresh cigarette. "If she lets her passion spend itself in silence it will pass the more swiftly."

Walking up and down he indulged in philosophic reflections concerning the useless emotionality of woman, and the duty of man not to be infected by it. . . . He grew quite warm in the proud consciousness of his heart's coldness.

Then suddenly—from the depth of the silence that was about him—resounded in a long-drawn, shrill, whirring voice that he had never heard— his own name.

"Rrricharrd!" it shrilled, stern and hard as the command of some paternal martinet. The voice seemed to come from subterranean depths.

He shivered and looked about. Nothing moved. There was no living soul in the next room.

"Richard!" the voice sounded a second time. This time the sound seemed but a few paces from him, but it arose from the ground as though a teasing goblin lay under his chair.

He bent over and peered into dark corners.

The mystery was solved: Joko, Alice's parrot, having secretly stolen from his quarters, sat on the rung of a chair and played the evil conscience of the house.

The tame animal stepped with dignity upon his outstretched hand and permitted itself to be lifted into the light. . . . Its glittering neck-feathers stood up, and while it whetted its beak on Niebeldingk's cuff-links, it repeated in a most subterranean voice: "Richard!"

And suddenly the dear feeling of belonging here, of being at home came over Niebeldingk. He had all but lost it. But its gentle power drew him on and refreshed him.

It was his right and his duty to be at home here where a dear woman lived so exclusively for him that the voice of her yearning sounded even from the tongue of the brute beast that she possessed! There was no possibility of feeling free and alien here.

"I must find her!" he thought quickly, "I musn't leave her alone another second."

He set Joko carefully on the table and sought to reach her bedroom which he had never entered by this approach.

In the door that led to the rear hall she met him. Her demeanour had its accustomed calm, her eyes were clear and dry.

"My poor, dear darling!" he cried and wanted to take her in his arms.

A strange, repelling glance met him and interrupted his beautiful emotion. Something hardened in him and he felt a new inclination to sarcasm.

"Forgive me for leaving you," she said, "one

must have patience with the folly of my sex. You know that well."

And she preceded him to his old place.

Screaming with pleasure Joko flew forward to meet her, and Niebeldingk remained standing to take his leave.

She did not hold him back.

Outside it occurred to him that he hadn't told her the anecdote of Fritz and the Indian lilies.

"It's a pity," he thought, "it might have cheered her." . . .

VIII.

NEXT morning Niebeldingk sat at his desk and reflected with considerable discomfort on the experience of the previous evening. Suddenly he observed, across the street, restlessly waiting in the same doorway—the avenging spirit!

It was an opportune moment. It would distract him to make an example of the fellow. Nothing better could have happened.

He rang for John and ordered him to bring up the wretched fellow and, furthermore, to hold himself in readiness for an act of vigorous expulsion.

Five minutes passed. Then the door opened and, diffidently, but with a kind of professional dignity, the knight of several honourable orders entered the room.

Niebeldingk made rapid observations: A beardless, weatherworn old face with pointed, stiff, white brows. The little, watery eyes knew how to hide their cunning, for nothing was visible in them save an expression of wonder and consternation. The black frock coat was threadbare but clean, his linen was spotless. He wore a stock which had been the last word of fashion at the time of the July revolution.

"A sharper of the most sophisticated sort," Niebeldingk concluded.

"Before any discussion takes place," he said sharply. "I must know with whom I am dealing."

The old man drew off with considerable difficulty his torn, gray, funereal gloves and, from the depths of a greasy pocket-book, produced a card which had, evidently, passed through a good many hands.

"A sharper," Niebeldingk repeated to himself, "but on a pretty low plane." He read the card: "Kohleman, retired clerk of court." And below was printed the addition: "Knight of several orders."

"What decorations have you?" he asked.

"I have been very graciously granted the Order of the Crown, fourth class, and the general order for good behaviour."

"Sit down," Niebeldingk replied, impelled by a slight instinctive respect.

"Thank you, I'll take the liberty," the old gentleman answered and sat down on the extreme edge of a chair.

"Once on the stairs you——" he was about to say "attacked me," but he repressed the words. "I know," he began, "what your business is. And now tell me frankly: Do you think any man in the world such a fool as to contemplate marriage because a frivolous young thing whose acquaintance he made at a supper given to 'cocottes' accompanies him, in the middle of the night, to his bachelor quarters? Do you think that a reasonable proposition?"

"No," the old gentleman answered with touching honesty. "But you know it's pretty discouraging to have Meta get into that kind of a mess. I've had my suspicions for some time that that baggage is a keener, and I've often said to my sister: 'Look here, these theatrical women are no proper company for a girl——' "

"Well then," Niebeldingk exclaimed, overcome with astonishment, "if that's the case, what are you after?"

"I?" the old gentleman quavered and pointed a funereal glove at his breast, "I? Oh, dear sakes alive! I'm not after anything. Do you imagine, my dear sir, that I get any fun out of tramping up and down in front of your house on my old legs? I'd rather sit in a corner and leave strange people to their own business. But what can I do? I live in my sister's house, and I do pay her a little board, for I'd never take a present, not a penny—that was never my way. But what I pay isn't much, you know, and so I have to make myself a bit useful in the boarding-house. The ladies have little errands, you know. And they're quite nice, too, except that they get as nasty as can be if their rooms aren't promptly cleaned in the morning, and so I help with the dusting, too. . . . If only it weren't for my asthma. . . . I tell, you, asthma, my dear sir——"

He stopped for an attack of coughing choked him.

With a sudden kindly emotion Niebeldingk regarded the terrible avenger in horror of whom he had lived four mortal days. He told him to stretch his poor old legs and asked him whether he'd like a glass of Madeira.

The old gentleman's face brightened. If it would surely give no trouble he would take the liberty of accepting.

Niebeldingk rang and John entered with a grand inquisitorial air. He recoiled when he saw the monster so comfortable and, for the first time in his service, permitted himself a gentle shake of the head.

The old gentleman emptied his glass in one gulp and wiped his mouth with a brownish cotton handkerchief. Fragments of tobacco flew about. He looked so tenderly at the destroyer of his family as though he had a sneaking desire to join the enemy.

"Well, well," he began again. "What's to be

done? If my sister takes something into her
head. . . . And anyhow, I'll tell you in confidence, she is a devil. Oh deary me, what I
have to put up with from her! It's no good
getting into trouble with her! . . . If you
want to avoid any unpleasantness, I can only
advise you to consent right away. . . . You
can back out later. . . . But that would be
the easiest way."

Niebeldingk laughed heartily.

"Yes, you can laugh," the old gentleman said
sadly, "that's because you don't know my sister."

"But *you* know her, my dear man. . . .
And do you suppose that she may have other,
that is to say, financial aims, while she——"

The old gentleman looked at him with great
scared eyes.

"How do you mean?" he said and crushed the
brown handkerchief in his hollow hand.

"Well, well, well," Niebeldingk quieted him
and poured a reconciling second glass of wine.

But he wasn't to be bribed.

"Permit me, my dear sir," he said, "but you
misunderstand me entirely. . . . Even if I
do help my sister in the house, and even if I do
go on errands, I would never have consented to
go on such an one. . . . I said to my sister:
It's marriage or nothing. . . . We don't go
in for blackmail, of that you may be sure."

"Well, my dear man," Niebeldingk laughed, "If that's the alternative, then—nothing!"

The old gentleman grew quite peaceable again.

"Goodness knows, you're quite right. But you will have unpleasantnesses. Mark my word. . . . And if she has to appeal to the Emperor, my sister said. And my sister—I mention it quite in confidence—my sister——"

"Is a devil, I understand."

"Exactly."

He laughed slyly as one who is getting even with an old enemy and drank, with every evidence of delight, the second glassful of wine.

Niebeldingk considered. Whether unfathomable stupidity or equally unfathomable sophistication lay at the bottom of all this—the business was a wretched one. It was just such an affair as would be dragged through every scandal mongering paper in the city, thoroughly equipped, of course, with the necessary moral decoration. He could almost see the heavy headlines: Rascality of a Nobleman.

"Yes, yes, my dear fellow," he said, and patted the terrible enemy's shoulder, "I tell you it's a dog's life. If you can avoid it any way—never go in for fast living."

The old gentleman shook his gray head sadly.

"That's all over," he declared, "but twenty years ago——"

Niebeldingk cut short the approaching confidences.

"Well, what's going to happen now?" he asked. "And what will your sister do when you come home and announce my refusal?"

"I'll tell you, Baron. In fact, my sister required that I *should* tell you, because that is to —" he giggled—"that is to have a profound effect. We've got a nephew, I must tell you, who's a lieutenant in the army. Well, he is to come at once and challenge you to a duel. . . . Well, now, a duel is always a pretty nasty piece of business. First, there's the scandal, and then, one *might* get hurt. And so my sister thought that you'd rather——"

"Hold on, my excellent friend," said Niebeldingk and a great weight rolled from his heart. "You have an officer in your family? That's splendid . . . I couldn't ask anything better . . . You wire him at once and tell him that I'll be at home three days running and ready to give him the desired explanations. I'm sorry for the poor fellow for being mixed up in such a stupid mess, but I can't help him."

"Why do you feel sorry for him?" the old gentleman asked. "He's as good a marksman as you are."

"Assuredly," Niebeldingk returned. "As-

suredly a better one . . . Only it won't
come to that."

He conducted his visitor with great ceremony
into the outer hall.

The latter remained standing for a moment in
the door. He grasped Niebeldingk's hand with
overflowing friendliness.

"My dear baron, you have been so nice to me
and so courteous. Permit me, in return, to offer
you an old man's counsel: Be more careful
about flowers!"

"What flowers?"

"Well, you sent a great, costly bunch of them.
That's what first attracted my sister's attention.
And when my sister gets on the track of any-
thing, well!" . . .

He shook with pleasure at the sly blow he
had thus delivered, drew those funereal gloves of
his from the crown of his hat and took his
leave.

"So it was the fault of the Indian lilies," Niebeldingk thought, looking after the queer old
knight with an amused imprecation. That
gentleman, enlivened by the wine he had taken,
pranced with a new flexibility along the side-
walk. "Like the count in *Don Juan*," Niebeldingk thought, "only newly equipped and
modernised."

The intervention of the young officer placed

the whole affair upon an intelligible basis. It remained only to treat it with entire seriousness.

Niebeldingk, according to his promise, remained at home until sunset for three boresome days. On the morning of the fourth he wrote a letter to the excellent old gentleman telling him that he was tired of waiting and requesting an immediate settlement of the business in question. Thereupon he received the following answer:

"SIR:—

In the name of my family I declare to you herewith that I give you over to the well-deserved contempt of your fellowmen. A man who can hesitate to restore the honour of a loving and yielding girl is not worthy of an alliance with our family. Hence we now sever any further connection with you.

With that measure of esteem which you deserve,

I am,

KOHLEMAN, *Retired Clerk of Court.*
Knight S. H. O.

P. S.

Best regards. Don't mind all that talk. The duel came to nothing. Our little lieutenant besought us not to ruin him and asked that his name be not mentioned. He has left town."

Breathing a deep sigh of relief, Niebeldingk threw the letter aside.

Now that the affair was about to float into

oblivion, he became aware of the fact that it had
weighed most heavily upon him.

And he began to feel ashamed.

He, a man who, by virtue of his name and of
his wealth and, if he would be bold, by virtue of
his intellect, was able to live in some noble and
distinguished way—he passed his time with
banalities that were half sordid and half humorous. These things had their place. Youth
might find them not unfruitful of experience.
They degraded a man of forty.

If these things filled his life to-day, then the
years of training and slow maturing had surely
gone for nothing. And what would become of
him if he carried these interests into his old age?
His schoolmates were masters of the great
sciences, distinguished servants of the government, influential politicians. They toiled in
the sweat of their brows and harvested the fruits
of their youth's sowing.

He strove to master these discomforting
thoughts, but every moment found him more defenceless against them.

And shame changed into disgust.

To divert himself he went out into the streets
and landed, finally, in the rooms of his club.
Here he was asked concerning his latest adventure. Only a certain respect which his personality inspired saved him from unworthy jests.

And in this poverty-stricken world, where the very lees of experience amounted to a sensation —here he wasted his days.

It must not last another week, not another day. So much suddenly grew clear to him.

He hurried away. Upon the streets brooded the heat of early summer. Masses of human beings, hot but happy, passed him in silent activity.

What was he to do?

He must marry: that admitted of no doubt. In the glow of his own hearth he must begin a new and more tonic life.

Marry? But whom? A worn out heart can no longer be made to beat more swiftly at the sight of some slim maiden. The senses might yet be stirred, but that is all.

Was he to haunt watering-places and pay court to mothers on the man-hunt in order to find favour in their daughters' eyes? Was he to travel from estate to estate and alienate the affection of young *chatelaines* from their favourite lieutenants?

Impossible!

He went home hopelessly enough and drowsed away the hours of the afternoon behind drawn blinds on a hot couch.

Toward evening the postman brought a letter —in Alice's hand.

Alice! How could he have forgotten her! His first duty should have been to see her.

He opened the envelope, warmly grateful for her mere existence.

"DEAR FRIEND:—

As you will probably not find time before you leave the city to bid me farewell in person, I beg you to return to me a certain key which I gave into your keeping some years ago. You have no need of it and it worries me to have it lying about.

Don't think that I am at all angry. My friendship and my gratitude are yours, however far and long we may be separated. When, some day, we meet again, we will both have become different beings. With many blessings upon your way,

ALICE."

He struck his forehead like a man who awakens from an obscene dream.

Where was his mind? He was about to go in search of that which was so close at hand, so richly his own!

Where else in all the world could he find a woman so exquisitely tempered to his needs, so intimately responsive to his desires, one who would lead him into the darker land of matrimony through meadows of laughing flowers?

To be sure, there was her coolness of temper,

her learning, her strange restlessness. But was not all that undergoing a change? Had he not found her sunk in dreams? And her tears? And her kiss?

Ungrateful wretch that he was!

He had sought a home and not thought of the parrot who screamed out his name in her dear dwelling. There was a parrot like that in the world—and he wandered foolishly abroad. What madness! What baseness!

He would go to her at once.

But no! A merry thought struck him and a healing one.

He took the key from the wall and put it into his pocket.

He would go to her—at midnight.

IX.

HE had definitely abandoned his club, the theatres were closed, the restaurants were deserted, his brother's family was in the country. . . . . It was not easy to pass the evening with that great resolve in his heart and that small key in his pocket.

Until ten he drifted about under the foliage of the *Tiergarten*. He listened to the murmur of couples who thronged the dark benches, regarded those who were quietly walking in the alleys and found himself, presently, in that stream of humanity which is drawn irresistibly toward the brightly illuminated pleasure resorts.

He was moved and happy at once. For the first time in years he felt himself to be a member of the family of man, a humbly serving brother in the commonweal of social purpose.

His time of proud, individualistic morality was over: the ever-blessing institution of the family was about to gather him to its hospitable bosom.

To be sure, his wonted scepticism was not utterly silenced. But he drove it away with a feeling of delighted comfort. He could have shouted a blessing to the married couples in search of air, he could have given a word of fatherly advice to the couples on the benches: "Children, commit no indiscretions—marry!"

And when he thought of her! A mild and peaceable tenderness of which he had never thought himself capable welled up from his arid heart. . . . Wide gardens of Paradise seemed to open, gardens with secret grottos and shady corners. And upon one of the palm-trees there sat Joko—amiable beast—and said: "Rrricharrrd!"

He went over the coming scene in his imagination again and again: Her little cry of panic when he would enter the dark room and then his whispered reassurance: "It is I, my darling. I have come back to stay for ever and ever."

And then happiness, gentle and heartfelt.

If a divorce was necessary, the relatives of her husband would probably succeed in divesting her of most of the property. What did it matter to either of them? Was he not rich and was she not sure of him? If need were, he could, with one stroke of the pen, repay her threefold all that she might lose. But, indeed, these reflections were quite futile. For when two people are so welded together in their souls, their earthly possessions need no separation.

From ten until half past eleven he sat in a corner of the *Café Bauer* and read the paper of his native province which, usually, he never looked at. With childlike delight he read into the local notices and advertisements things pertinent to his future life.

Bremsel, the delicatessen man in a neighbouring town advertised fresh crabs. And Alice liked them. "Splendid," he thought "we won't have to bring them from far." And suddenly he himself felt an appetite for the shell-fish, so thoroughly had he lived himself into his vision of domestic felicity.

At twenty-five minutes of twelve he paid for his chartreuse and set out on foot. He had time to spare and he did not want to cause the unavoidable disturbance of a cab's stopping at her door.

The house, according to his hope, was dark and silent.

With beating heart he drew forth the key which consisted of two collapsible parts. One part was for the house door, the other for a door in her bed-room that led to a separate entrance. He had himself chosen the apartment with this advantage in view.

He passed the lower hall unmolested and reached the creaking stairs which he had always hated. And as he mounted he registered an oath to pass this way no more. He would not thus jeopardise the fair fame of his betrothed.

It would be bad enough if he had to rap, in case the night latch was drawn. . . .

The outer door, at least, offered no difficulty. He touched it and it swung loose on its hinges.

For a moment the mad idea came into his head that—in answer to her letter—Alice might have foreseen the possibility of his coming. . . . He was just about to test, by a light pressure, the knob of the inner door when, coming from the bed-room, a muffled sound of speech reached his ear.

One voice was Alice's: the other—his breath stopped. It was not the maid's. He knew it well. It was the voice of Fritz von Ehrenberg.

It was over then—for him. . . . And again and again he murmured: "It's all over."

He leaned weakly against the wall.

Then he listened.

This woman who could not yield with sufficient fervour to the abandon of passionate speech and action—this was Alice, his Alice, with her fine sobriety, her philosophic clearness of mind.

And that young fool whose mouth she closed with long kisses of gratitude for his folly—did he realise the blessedness which had fallen to the lot of his crude youth?

It was over . . . all over.

And he was so worn, so passionless, so autumnal of soul, that he could smile wearily in the midst of his pain.

Very carefully he descended the creaking stairs, locked the door of the house and stood on the street—still smiling.

It was over . . . all over.

Her future was trodden into the mire, hers and his own.

And in this supreme moment he grew cruelly aware of his crimes against her.

All her love, all her being during these years had been but one secret prayer: "Hold me, do not break me, do not desert me!"

He had been deaf. He had given her a stone for bread, irony for love, cold doubt for warm, human trust! And in the end he had even despised her because she had striven, with touching faith, to form herself according to his example.

It was all fatally clear—now.

Her contradictions, her lack of feeling, her haughty scepticism—all that had chilled and estranged him had been but a dutiful reflection of his own being.

Need he be surprised that the last remnant of her lost and corrupted youth rose in impassioned rebellion against him and, thinking to save itself, hurled itself to destruction?

He gave one farewell glance to the dark, silent house—the grave of the fairest hopes of all his life. Then he set out upon long, dreary, aimless wandering through the endless, nocturnal streets.

Like shadows the shapes of night glided by him.

Shy harlots—loud roysterers—benzin flames —more harlots—and here and there one lost in thought even as he.

An evil odour, as of singed horses' hoofs, floated over the city. . . . . The dust whirled under the street-cleaning machines.

The world grew silent. He was left almost alone. . . . .

Then the life of the awakening day began to stir. A sleepy dawn crept over the roofs. . . .

It was the next morning.

There would be no "next mornings" for him. That was over.

Let others send Indian lilies!

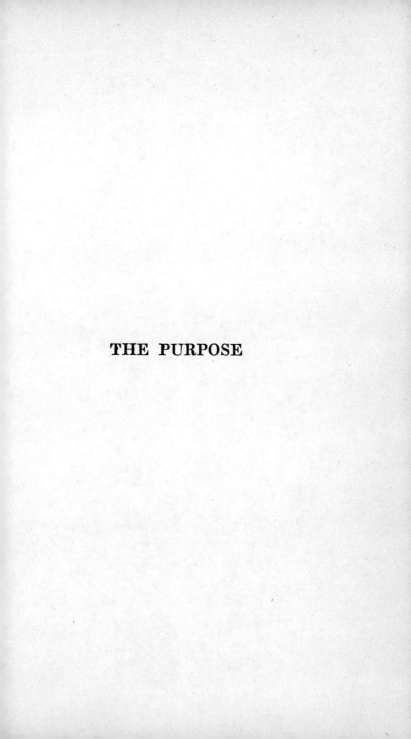

THE PURPOSE

THE PURPOSE

I.

It was a blazing afternoon, late in July. The Cheruskan fraternity entered Ellerntal in celebration of their mid-summer festivity. They had let the great wagon stand at the outskirts of the village and now marched up its street in well-formed procession, proud and vain as a company of *Schützen* before whom all the world bows down once a year.

First came the regimental band of the nearest garrison, dressed in civilian's clothes—then, under the vigilance of two brightly attired freshmen, the blue, white and golden banner of the fraternity, next the officers accompanied by other freshmen, and finally the active members in whom the dignity, decency and fighting strength of the fraternity were embodied. A gay little crowd of elderly gentlemen, ladies and guests followed in less rigid order. Last came, as always and everywhere, the barefoot children of the village.

The procession came to a halt in front of the *Prussian Eagle,* a long-drawn single story structure of frame. The newly added dance hall with its three great windows protruded loftily above the house.

The banner was lowered, the horns of the band gave wild, sharp signals to which no one attended, and Pastor Rhode, a sedate man of fifty dressed in the scarf and slashed cap of the order, stepped from the inn door to pronounce the address of welcome. At this moment it happened that one of the two banner bearers who had stood at the right and left of the flag with naked foils, rigid as statues, slowly tilted over forward and buried his face in the green sward.

This event naturally put an immediate end to the ceremony. Everybody, men and women, thronged around the fallen youth and were quickly pushed back by the medical fraternity men who were present in various stages of professional development.

The medical wisdom of this many-headed council culminated in the cry: "A glass of water!"

Immediately a young girl—hot-eyed and loose-haired, exquisite in the roundedness of half maturity—rushed out of the door and handed a glass to the gentlemen who had turned the fainting lad on his back and were loosening scarf and collar.

He lay there, in the traditional garb of the fraternity, like a young cavalry man of the time of the Great Elector—with his blue, gold-braided doublet, close-fitting breeches of white leather and mighty boots whose flapping tops swelled out over his firm thighs. He couldn't be above eighteen or nineteen, long and broad though he was, with his cheeks of milk and blood, that showed no sign of down, no duelling scar. You would have thought him some mother's pet, had there not been a sharp line of care that ran mournfully from the half-open lips to the chin.

The cold water did its duty. Sighing, the lad opened his eyes—two pretty blue boy's eyes, long lashed and yet a little empty of expression as though life had delayed giving them the harder glow of maturity.

These eyes fell upon the young girl who stood there, with hands pressed to her heaving bosom, in an ecstatic desire to help.

"Where can we carry him?" asked one of the physicians.

"Into my room," she cried, "I'll show you the way."

Eight strong hands took hold and two minutes later the boy lay on the flowered cover of her bed. It was far too short for him, but it stood, soft and comfortable, hidden by white mull curtains in a corner of her simple room.

He was summoned back to full consciousness, tapped, auscultated and examined. Finally he confessed with a good deal of hesitation that his right foot hurt him a bit—that was all.

"Are the boots your own, freshie?" asked one of the physicians.

He blushed, turned his gaze to the wall and shook his head.

Everyone smiled.

"Well, then, off with the wretched thing."

But all exertion of virile strength was in vain. The boot did not budge. Only a low moan of suffering came from the patient.

"There's nothing to be done," said one, "little miss, let's have a bread-knife."

Anxious and with half-folded hands she had stood behind the doctors. Now she rushed off and brought the desired implement.

"But you're not going to hurt him?" she asked with big, beseeching eyes.

"No, no, we're only going to cut his leg off," jested one of the by-standers and took the knife from her clinging fingers.

Two incisions, two rents along the shin—the leather parted. A steady surgeon's hand guided the knife carefully over the instep. At last the flesh appeared—bloody, steel-blue **and** badly swollen.

"Freshie, you idiot, you might have killed yourself," said the surgeon and gave the patient a paternal nudge. "And now, little miss, hurry —sugar of lead bandages till evening."

II.

HER name was Antonie. She was the inn-keeper Wiesner's only daughter and managed the household and kitchen because her mother had died in the previous year.

His name was Robert Messerschmidt. He was a physician's son and a student of medicine. He hoped to fight his way into full fraternity membership by the beginning of the next semester. This last detail was, at present, the most important of his life and had been confided to her at the very beginning of their acquaint-anceship.

Youth is in a hurry. At four o'clock their hands were intertwined. At five o'clock their lips found each other. From six on the bandages were changed more rarely. Instead they exchanged vows of eternal fidelity. At eight a solemn betrothal took place. And when, at ten o'clock, swaying slightly and mellow of mood, the physicians reappeared in order to put the patient to bed properly, their wedding-day had been definitely set for the fifth anniversary of that day.

Next morning the procession went on to cele-
brate in some other picturesque locality the
festival of the breakfast of "the morning after."

Toni had run up on the hill which ascended,
behind her father's house, toward the high
plateau of the river-bank. With dry but burning eyes she looked after the wagons which
gradually vanished in the silvery sand of the
road and one of which carried away into the
distance her life's whole happiness.

To be sure, she had fallen in love with everyone whom she had met. This habit dated from
her twelfth, nay, from her tenth year. But this
time it was different, oh, so different. This time
it was like an axe-blow from which one doesn't
arise. Or like the fell disease—consumption—
which had dragged her mother to the grave.

She herself was more like her father, thick-set,
and sturdy.

She had also inherited his calculating and
planning nature. With tough tenacity he could
sacrifice years of earning and saving and planning to acquire farms and meadows and or-
chards. Thus the girl could meditate and plan
her fate which, until yesterday, had been fluid as
water but which to-day lay definitely anchored
in the soul of a stranger lad.

Her education had been narrow. She knew
the little that an old governess and a comfort-

able pastor could teach. But she read whatever she could get hold of—from the tattered "pony" to Homer which a boy friend had loaned her, to the most horrible penny-dreadfuls which were her father's delight in his rare hours of leisure.

And she assimilated what she read and adapted it to her own fate. Thus her imagination was familiar with happiness, with delusion, with crime. . . .

She knew that she was beautiful. If the humility of her play-fellows had not assured her of this fact, she would have been enlightened by the long glances and jesting admiration of her father's guests.

Her father was strict. He interfered with ferocity if a traveller jested with her too intimately. Nevertheless he liked to have her come into the inn proper and slip, smiling and curtsying, past the wealthier guests. It was not unprofitable.

Upon his short, fleshy bow-legs, with his suspiciously calculating blink, with his avarice and his sharp tongue, he stood between her and the world, permitting only so much of it to approach her as seemed, at a given moment, harmless and useful.

His attitude was fatal to any free communication with her beloved. He opened and read every letter that she had ever received. Had she ventured to call for one at the post-office, the information would have reached him that very day.

The problem was how to deceive him without placing herself at the mercy of some friend.

She sat down in the arbour from which, past the trees of the orchard and the neighbouring river, one had a view of the Russian forests, and put the problem to her seventeen-year old brain. And while the summer wind played with the green fruit on the boughs and the white herons spread their gleaming wings over the river, she thought out a plan—the first of many by which she meant to rivet her beloved for life.

On the same afternoon she asked her father's permission to invite the daughter of the county-physician to visit her.

"Didn't know you were such great friends," he said, surprised.

"Oh, but we are," she pretended to be a little hurt. "We were received into the Church at the same time."

With lightning-like rapidity he computed the advantages that might result from such a visit. The county-seat was four miles distant and if the societies of veterans and marksmen in whose committees the doctor was influential could be persuaded to come hither for their outings. . . .

The girl was cordially invited and arrived a week later. She was surprised and touched to find so faithful a friend in Toni who, when they were both boarding with Pastor Rhode, had played her many a sly trick.

Two months later the girl, in her turn, invited Toni to the city whither she had never before been permitted to go alone and so the latter managed to receive her lover's first letter.

What he wrote was discouraging enough. His father was ill, hence the excellent practice was gliding into other hands and the means for his own studies were growing narrow. If things went on so he might have to give up his university course and take to anything to keep his mother and sister from want.

This prospect did not please Toni. She was so proud of him. She could not bear to have him descend in the social scale for the sake of bread and butter. She thought and thought how she could help him with money, but nothing occurred to her. She had to be content with encouraging him and assuring him that her love would find ways and means for helping him out of his difficulties.

She wrote her letters at night and jumped out of the window in order to drop them secretly into the pillar box. It was months before she could secure an answer. His father was better, but life in the fraternity was very expensive, and it was a very grave question whether he had not better resign the scarf which he had just gained and study on as a mere "barb."

In Toni's imagination the picture of her beloved was brilliantly illuminated by the glory of the tricoloured fraternity scarf, his desire for it had become so ardently her own, that she could not bear the thought of him—his yearning satisfied—returning to the gray commonplace garb of Philistia. And so she wrote him.

Spring came and Toni matured to statelier maidenhood. The plump girl, half-child, droll and naïve, grew to be a thoughtful, silent young woman, secretive and very sure of her aims. She condescended to the guests and took no notice of the desperate admiration which surrounded her. Her glowing eyes looked into emptiness, her infinitely tempting mouth smiled carelessly at friends and strangers.

In May Robert's father died.

She read it in one of the papers that were taken at the inn, and immediately it became clear to her that her whole future was at stake. For if he was crushed now by the load of family cares, if hope were taken from him, no thought of her or her love would be left. Only if she could redeem her promises and help him practically could she hope to keep him.

In the farthest corner of a rarely opened drawer lay her mother's jewels which were some day to be hers—brooches and rings, a golden chain, and a comb set with rubies which had found its way—heaven knows how—into the simple inn.

Without taking thought she stole the whole and sent it as merchandise—not daring to risk the evidence of registration—to help him in his studies. The few hundred marks that the jewellery would bring would surely keep him until the end of the semester . . . but what then? . . .

And again she thought and planned all through the long, hot nights.

Pastor Rhode's eldest son, a frail, tall junior who followed her, full of timid passion, came home from college for the spring vacation. In the dusk he crept around the inn as had been his wont for years.

This time he had not long to wait.

How did things go at college? Badly. Would he enter the senior class at Michaelmas? Hardly. Then she would have to be ashamed of him, and that would be a pity: she liked him too well.

The slim lad writhed under this exquisite torture. It wasn't his fault. He had pains in his chest, and growing pains. And all that.

She unfolded her plan.

"You ought to have a tutor during the long vacation, Emil, to help you work."

"Papa can do that."

"Oh, Papa is busy. You ought to have a tutor all to yourself, a student or something like that. If you're really fond of me ask your Papa to engage one. Perhaps he'll get a young man from his own fraternity with whom he can chat in the evening. You will ask, won't you? I don't like people who are conditioned in their studies."

That same night a letter was sent to her beloved.

"Watch the frat. bulletin! Our pastor is going to look for a tutor for his boy. See to it that you get the position. I'm longing to see you."

III.

ONCE more it was late July—exactly a year after those memorable events—and he sat in the stage-coach and took off his crape-hung cap to her. His face was torn by fresh scars and diagonally across his breast the blue white golden scarf was to be seen.

She grasped the posts of the fence with both hands and felt that she would die if she could not have him.

Upon that evening she left the house no more, although for two hours he walked the dusty village street, with Emil, but also alone. But on the next evening she stood behind the fence. Their hands found each other across the obstacle.

"Do you sleep on the ground-floor?" she asked whispering.

"Yes."

"Does the dog still bark when he sees you."

"I don't know, I'm afraid so."

"When you've made friends with him so that he won't bark when you get out of the window, then come to the arbour behind our orchard. I'll wait for you every night at twelve. But don't mind that. Don't come till you're sure of the dog."

For three long nights she sat on the wooden bench of the arbour until the coming of dawn and stared into the bluish dusk that hid the village as in a cloak. From time to time the dogs bayed. She could distinguish the bay of the pastor's collie. She knew his hoarse voice. Perhaps he was barring her beloved's way. . . .

At last, during the fourth night, when his coming was scarcely to be hoped for, uncertain steps dragged up the hill.

She did not run to meet him. She crouched in the darkest corner of the arbour and tasted, intensely blissful, the moments during which he felt his way through the foliage.

Then she clung to his neck, to his lips, demanding and according all—rapt to the very peaks of life. . . .

They were together nightly. Few words passed between them. She scarcely knew how he looked. For not even a beam of the moon could penetrate the broad-leaved foliage, and at the peep of dawn they separated. She might have lain in the arms of a stranger and not known the difference.

And not only during their nightly meetings, but even by day they slipt through life-like shadows.

One day the pastor came to the inn for a glass of beer and chatted with other gentlemen. She heard him.

"I don't know what's the matter with that young fellow," he said. "He does his duty and my boy is making progress. But he's like a stranger from another world. He sits at the table and scarcely sees us. He talks and you have the feeling that he doesn't know what he's talking about. Either he's anæmic or he writes poetry."

She herself saw the world through a blue veil, heard the voices of life across an immeasurable distance and felt hot, alien shivers run through her enervated limbs.

The early Autumn approached and with it the day of his departure. At last she thought of discussing the future with him which, until then, like all else on earth, had sunk out of sight.

His mother, he told her, meant to move to Koenigsberg and earn her living by keeping boarders. Thus there was at least a possibility of his continuing his studies. But he didn't believe that he would be able to finish. His present means would soon be exhausted and he had no idea where others would come from.

All that he told her in the annoyed and almost tortured tones of one long weary of hope who only staggers on in fear of more vital degradation.

With flaming words she urged him to be of good courage. She insisted upon such resources as—however frugal—were, after all, at hand, and calculated every penny. She shrugged her shoulders at his gratitude for that first act of helpfulness. If only there were something else to be taken. But whence and how? Her suspicious father would have observed any shortage in his till at once and would have had the thief discovered.

The great thing was to gain time. Upon her advice he was to leave Koenigsberg with its expensive fraternity life and pass the winter in Berlin. The rest had to be left to luck and cunning.

In a chill, foggy September night they said farewell. Shivering they held each other close. Their hearts were full of the confused hopes which they themselves had kindled, not because there was any ground for hope, but because without it one cannot live.

And a few weeks later everything came to an end.

For Toni knew of a surety that she would be a mother. . . .

IV.

INTO the river!

For that her father would put her in the street
was clear. It was equally clear what would become of her in that case. . . .

But no, not into the river! Why was her
young head so practised in skill and cunning, if
it was to bow helplessly under the first severe on-
slaught of fate? What was the purpose of those
beautiful long nights but to brood upon plans
and send far thoughts out toward shining aims?

No, she would not run into the river. That
dear wedding-day in five, nay, in four years, was
lost anyhow. But the long time could be utilised
so cleverly that her beloved could be dragged
across the abyss of his fate.

First, then, she must have a father for her
child. He must not be clever. He must not be
strong of will. Nor young, for youth makes demands. . . . Nor well off, for he who is
certain of himself desires freedom of choice.

Her choice fell upon a former inn-keeper, a
down-hearted man of about fifty, moist of eye,
faded, with greasy black hair. . . . He had

failed in business some years before and now sat around in the inn, looking for a job. . . .

To this her father did not object. For that man's condition was an excellent foil to his own success and prosperity and thus he was permitted, at times, to stay a week in the house where, otherwise, charity was scarcely at home.

Her plan worked well. On the first day she lured him silently on. On the second he responded. On the third she turned sharply and rebuked him. On the fourth she forgave him. On the fifth she met him in secret. On the sixth he went on a journey, conscience smitten for having seduced her. . . .

That very night—for there was no time to be lost—she confessed with trembling and blushing to her father that she was overcome by an unconquerable passion for Herr Weigand. As was to be expected she was driven from the door with shame and fury.

During the following weeks she went about bathed in tears. Her father avoided her. Then, when the right moment seemed to have come, she made a second and far more difficult confession. This time her tremours and her blushes were real, her tears were genuine for her father used a horse-whip. . . . But when, that night, Toni sat on the edge of her bed and bathed the

bloody welts on her body, she knew that her plan
would succeed.

And, to be sure, two days later Herr Weigand
returned—a little more faded, a little more hesitant, but altogether, by no means unhappy. He
was invited into her father's office for a long
discussion. The result was that the two lovers
fell into each others' arms while her father,
trembling with impotent rage, hurled at them the
fragments of a crushed cigar.

The banns were proclaimed immediately after
the bethrothal, and a month later Herr Weigand, in his capacity of son-in-law, could take
possession of the same garret which he had inhabited as an impecunious guest. This arrange-
ment, however, was not a permanent one. An
inn was to be rented for the young couple—
with her father's money.

Toni, full of zeal and energy, took part in
every new undertaking, travelled hither and
thither, considered prospects and dangers, but
always withdrew again at the last moment in
order to await a fairer opportunity.

But she was utterly set upon the immediate
furnishing of the new home. She went to
Koenigsberg and had long sessions with furniture dealers and tradesmen of all kinds. On account of her delicate condition she insisted that
she could only travel on the upholstered seats of

the second class. She charged her father accordingly and in reality travelled fourth class and sat for hours between market-women and Polish Jews in order to save a few marks. In the accounts she rendered heavy meals were itemized, strengthening wines, stimulating cordials. As a matter of fact, she lived on dried slices of bread which, before leaving home, she hid in her trunk.

She did not disdain the saving of a tram car fare, although the rebates which she got on the furniture ran into the hundreds.

All that she sent jubilantly to her lover in Berlin, assured that he was provided for some months.

Thus the great misfortune had finally resulted in a blessing. For, without these unhoped for resources, he must have long fallen by the wayside.

Months passed. Her furnishings stood in a storage warehouse, but the house in which they were to live was not yet found.

When she felt that her hour had come—her father and husband thought it far off—she redoubled the energy of her travels, seeking, preferably, rough and ribbed roads which other women in her condition were wont to shun.

And thus, one day, in a springless vehicle, two miles distant from the county-seat, the pains of labour came upon her. She steeled every nerve and had herself carried to the house of the county-physician whose daughter was now tenderly attached to her.

There she gave birth to a girl child which announced its equivocal arrival in this world lustily.

The old doctor, into whose house this confusion had suddenly come, stood by her bed-side, smiling good-naturedly. She grasped him with both hands, terror in her eyes and in her voice.

" Dear, dear doctor! The baby was born too soon, wasn't it?"

The doctor drew back and regarded her long and earnestly. Then his smile returned and his kind hand touched her hair.

"Yes, it is as you say. The baby's nails are not fully developed and its weight is slightly below normal. It's all on account of your careless rushing about. Surely the child came too soon."

And he gave her the proper certification of the fact which protected her from those few people who might consider themselves partakers of her secret. For the opinion of people in general she cared little. So strong had she grown through guilt and silence.

And she was a child of nineteen! . . .

V.

WHEN Toni had arisen from her bed of pain she found the place which she and her husband had been seeking for months with surprising rapidity. The "Hotel Germania," the most reputable hotel in the county-seat itself was for rent. Its owner had recently died. It was palatial compared to her father's inn. There were fifteen rooms for guests, a tap-room, a wine-room, a grocery-shop and a livery-stable.

Weigand, intimidated by misfortune, had never even hoped to aspire to such heights of splendour. Even now he could only grasp the measure of his happiness by calculating enormous profits. And he did this with peculiar delight. For, since the business was to be run in the name of Toni's father, his own creditors could not touch him.

When they had moved in and the business began to be straightened out, Weigand proved himself in flat contradiction of his slack and careless character, a tough and circumspect man of business. He knew the whereabouts of every penny and was not inclined to permit his wife to make random inroads upon his takings.

Toni, who had expected to be undisputed mistress of the safe saw herself cheated of her dearest hopes, for the time approached when the savings made on the purchase of her furniture must necessarily be exhausted.

And again she planned and wrestled through the long, warm nights while her husband, whose inevitable proximity she bore calmly, snored with the heaviness of many professional "treats."

One day she said to him: "A few pennies must be put by for Amanda." That was the name of the little girl who flourished merrily in her cradle. "You must assign some little profits to me."

"What can I do?" he asked. "For the present everything belongs to the old man."

"I know what I'd like," she went on, smiling dreamily, "I'd like to have all the profits on the sale of champagne."

He laughed heartily. There wasn't much call for champagne in the little county-seat. At most a few bottles were sold on the emperor's birthday or when, once in a long while, a flush commercial traveller wanted to regale a recalcitrant customer.

And so Weigand fell in with what he thought a mere mood and assented.

Toni at once made a trip to Koenigsberg and bought all kinds of phantastic decorations—

Chinese lanterns, gilt fans, artificial flowers, gay vases and manicoloured lamp-shades. With all these things she adorned the little room that lay behind the room in which the most distinguished townspeople were wont to drink their beer. And so the place with veiled light and crimson glow looked more like a mysterious oriental shrine than the sitting-room of an honest Prussian inn-keeper's wife.

She sat evening after evening in this phantastic room. She brought her knitting and awaited the things that were to come.

The gentlemen who drank in the adjoining room, the judges, physicians, planters—all the bigwigs of a small town, in short—soon noticed the magical light that glimmered through the half-open door whenever Weigand was obliged to pass from the public rooms into his private dwelling. And the men grew to be curious, the more so as the inn-keeper's young wife, of whose charms many rumours were afloat, had never yet been seen by any.

One evening, when the company was in an especially hilarious mood, the men demanded stormily to see the mysterious room.

Weigand hesitated. He would have to ask his wife's permission. He returned with the friendly message that the gentlemen were welcome. Hesitant, almost timid, they entered as if crossing the threshold of some house of mystery.

There stood—transfigured by the glow of coloured lamps—the shapely young woman with the alluring glow in her eyes, and her lips that were in the form of a heart. She gave each a secretly quivering hand and spoke a few soft words that seemed to distinguish him from the others. Then, still timid and modest, she asked them to be seated and begged for permission to serve a glass of champagne in honour of the occasion.

It is not recorded who ordered the second bottle. It may have been the very fat Herr von Loffka, or the permanently hilarious judge. At all events the short visit of the gentlemen came to an end at three o'clock in the morning with wild intoxication and a sale of eighteen bottles of champagne, of which half bore French labels.

Toni resisted all requests for a second invitation to her sanctum. She first insisted on the solemn assurance that the gentlemen would respect her presence and bring neither herself nor her house into ill-repute. At last came the imperial county-counsellor himself—a wealthy bachelor of fifty with the manners of an injured lady killer. He came to beg for himself and the others and she dared not refuse any longer.

The champagne festivals continued. With

this difference: that Toni, whenever the atmosphere reached a certain point of heated intoxication, modestly withdrew to her bedroom. Thus she succeeded not only in holding herself spotless but in being praised for her retiring nature.

But she kindled a fire in the heads of these dissatisfied University men who deemed themselves banished into a land of starvation, and in the senses of the planters' sons. And this fire burned on and created about her an atmosphere of madly fevered desire. . . .

Finally it became the highest mark of distinction in the little town, the sign of real connoisseurship in life, to have drunk a bottle of champagne with "Germania," as they called her, although she bore greater resemblance to some swarthier lady of Rome. Whoever was not admitted to her circle cursed his lowliness and his futile life.

Of course, in spite of all precautions, it could not but be that her reputation suffered. The daughter of the county-physician began to avoid her, the wives of social equals followed suit. But no one dared accuse her of improper relations with any of her adorers. It was even known that the county-counsellor, desperate over her stern refusals, was urging her to get a divorce from her husband and marry him. No one suspected, of course, that she had herself spread this ru-

mour in order to render pointless the possible
leaking out of improprieties. . . .

Nor did any one dream that a bank in Koenigsberg transmitted, in her name, monthly cheques
to Berlin that sufficed amply to help an ambitious
medical student to continue his work.

The news which she received from her beloved
was scanty.

In order to remain in communication with him
she had thought out a subtle method.

The house of every tradesman or business man
in the provinces is flooded with printed advertisements from Berlin which pour out over the
small towns and the open country. Of this
printed matter, which is usually thrown aside
unnoticed, Toni gathered the most voluminous
examples, carefully preserved the envelopes, and
sent them to Robert. Her husband did not
notice of course that the same advertising matter
came a second time nor that faint, scarce legible
pencil marks picked out words here and there
which, when read consecutively, made complete
sense and differed very radically from the message which the printed slips were meant to convey. . . .

Years passed. A few ship-wrecked lives
marked Toni's path, a few female slanders
against her were avenged by the courts. Otherwise nothing of import took place.

And in her heart burned with never-lessening glow the one great emotion which always supplied fuel to her will, which lent every action a pregnant significance and furnished absolution for every crime.

In the meantime Amanda grew to be a blue-eyed, charming child—gentle and caressing and the image of the man of whose love she was the impassioned gift.

But Fate, which seems to play its gigantic pranks upon men in the act of punishing them, brought it to pass that the child seemed also to bear some slight resemblance to the stranger who, bowed and servile, stupidly industrious, sucking cigars, was to be seen at her mother's side.

Never was father more utterly devoted to the fruit of his loins than this gulled fellow to the strange child to whom the mother did not even— by kindly inactivity—give him a borrowed right. The more carefully she sought to separate the child from him, the more adoringly and tenaciously did he cling to it.

With terror and rage Toni was obliged to admit to herself that no sum would ever suffice to make Weigand agree to a divorce that separated him definitely from the child. And dreams and visions, transplanted into her brain from evil books, filled Toni's nights with the glitter of daggers and the stain of flowing blood. And fate seemed to urge on the day when these dreams must take on flesh. . . .

One day she found in the waste-paper basket which she searched carefully after every mail-delivery, an advertisement which commended to the buying public a new make of type-writer.

"Many public institutions," thus the advertisement ran, "use our well tried machines in their offices, because these machines will bear the most rigid examination. Their reputation has crossed the ocean. The Chilean ministry has just ordered a dozen of our 'Excelsiors' by cable. Thus successfully does our invention spread over the world. And yet its victorious progress is by no means completed. Even in Japan——" and so on.

If one looked at this stuff very carefully, one could observe that certain words were lightly marked in pencil. And if one read these words consecutively, the following sentence resulted: "Public—examination—just—successfully—completed."

From this day on the room with the veiled lamps remained closed to her eager friends. From this day on the generous county-counsellor saw that his hopes were dead. . . .

VI.

How was the man to be disposed of?

An open demand for divorce would have been stupid, for it would have thrown a very vivid suspicion upon any later and more drastic attempt.

Weigand's walk and conversation were blameless. Her one hope consisted in catching him in some chance infidelity. The desire for change, she reasoned, the allurement of forbidden fruit, must inflame even this wooden creature.

She had never, hitherto, paid the slightest attention to the problem of waitresses. Now she travelled to Koenigsberg and hired the handsomest women to be found in the employment bureaus. They came, one after another, a feline Polish girl, a smiling, radiantly blond child of Sweden—a Venus, a Germania—this time a genuine one. Next came a pretended Circassian princess. And they all wandered off again, and Weigand had no glance for them but that of the master.

Antonie was discouraged and dropped her plan.

What now?

She had recoiled from no baseness. She had sacrificed to her love honour, self-respect, truth, righteousness and pride. But she had avoided hitherto the possibility of a conflict with the law. Occasional small thefts in the house did not count.

But the day had come when crime itself, crime that threatened remorse and the sword of judgment, entered her life. For otherwise she could not get rid of her husband.

The regions that lie about the eastern boundary of the empire are haunted by Jewish peddlers who carry in their sacks Russian drops, candied fruits, gay ribands, toys made of bark, and other pleasant things which make them welcome to young people. But they also supply sterner needs. In the bottom of their sacks are hidden love philtres and strange electuaries. And if you press them very determinedly, you will find some among them who have the little white powders that can be poured into beer . . . or the small, round discs which the common folk call "crow's eyes" and which the greedy apothecaries will not sell you merely for the reason that they prepare the costlier strychnine from them.

You will often see these beneficent men in the twilight in secret colloquy with female figures by garden-gates and the edges of woods. The female figures slip away if you happen to appear on the road. . . . Often, too, these men are asked into the house and intimate council is held with them—especially when husband and servants are busy in the fields. . . .

One evening in the beginning of May, Toni brought home with her from a harmless walk a little box of arsenic and a couple of small, hard discs that rattled merrily in one's pocket. . . . Cold sweat ran down her throat and her legs trembled so that she had to sit down on a case of soap before entering the house.

Her husband asked her what was wrong.

"Ah, it's the spring," she answered and laughed.

Soon her adorers noticed, and not these only, that her loveliness increased from day to day. Her eyes which, under their depressed brows, had assumed a sharp and peering gaze, once more glowed with their primal fire, and a warm rosiness suffused her cheeks that spread marvelously to her forehead and throat.

Her appearance made so striking an impression that many a one who had not seen her for a space stared at her and asked, full of admiration: "What have you done to yourself?"

"It is the spring," she answered and laughed.

As a matter of fact she had taken to eating arsenic.

She had been told that any one who becomes

accustomed to the use of this poison can increase the doses to such an extent that he can take without harm a quantity that will necessarily kill another. And she had made up her mind to partake of the soup which she meant, some day, to prepare for her husband. That much she held to be due a faultless claim of innocence.

But she was unfortunate enough to make a grievous mistake one day, and lay writhing on the floor in uncontrollable agony.

The old physician at once recognized the symptoms of arsenic poisoning, prescribed the necessary antidotes and carefully dragged her back into life. The quantity she had taken, he declared, shaking his head, was enough to slay a strong man. He transmitted the information of the incident as demanded by law.

Detectives and court-messengers visited the house. The entire building was searched, documents had to be signed and all reports were carefully followed up.

The dear romantic public refused to be robbed of its opinion that one of Toni's rejected admirers had thus sought to avenge himself. The suspicion of the authorities, however, fastened itself upon a waitress, a plump, red-haired wanton who had taken the place of the imported beauties and whose insolent ugliness the men of the town, relieved of nobler delights, enjoyed thoroughly. The insight of the investigating judge had found in the girl's serving in the house and her apparent intimacy with its master a scent which he would by no means abandon. Only, because a few confirmatory details were still to seek, the suspicion was hidden not only from the public but even from its object.

Antonie, however, ailed continually. She grew thin, her digestion was delicate. If the blow was to be struck—and many circumstances urged it —she would no longer be able to share the poison with her victim. But it seemed fairly certain that suspicion would very definitely fall not upon her but upon the other woman. The latter would have to be sacrificed, so much was clear.

But that was the difficulty. The wounded conscience might recover, the crime might be conquered into forgetfulness, if only that is slain which burdens the earth, which should never have been. But Toni felt that her soul could not drag itself to any bourne of peace if, for her own advantage, she cast one who was innocent to lasting and irremediable destruction.

The simplest thing would have been to dismiss the woman. In that case, however, it was possible that the courts would direct their investigations to her admirers. One of them had spoken hasty and careless words. He might not be able to clear himself, were the accusation directed against him.

There remained but one hope: to ascribe the unavertible death of her husband to some accident, some heedlessness. And so she directed her unwavering purpose to this end.

The Polish peddler had slipped into Toni's hand not only the arsenic but also the deadly little discs called "crows eyes." These must help her, if used with proper care and circumspection.

One day while little Amanda was playing in the yard with other girls, she found among the empty kerosene barrels a few delightful, silvery discs, no larger then a ten pfennig piece. With great delight she brought them to her mother who, attending to her knitting, had ceased for a moment to watch the children.

"What's that, Mama?"

"I don't know, my darling."

"May we play with them?"

"What would you like to play?"

"We want to throw them."

"No, don't do that. But I'll make you a new doll-carriage and these will be lovely wheels."

The children assented and Amanda brought a pair of scissors in order to make holes in the little wheels. But they were too hard and the points of the blades slipped.

"Ask father to use his small gimlet."

Amanda ran to the open window behind which he for whom all this was prepared was quietly making out his monthly bills.

Toni's breath failed. If he recognised the poisonous fruits, it was all over with her plan. But the risk was not to be avoided.

He looked at the discs for a moment. And yet for another. No, he did not know their nature but was rather pleased with them. It did not even occur to him to warn the little girl to beware of the unknown fruit.

He called into the shop ordering an apprentice to bring him a tool-case. The boy in his blue apron came and Toni observed that his eyes rested upon the fruits for a perceptible interval. Thus there was, in addition to the children, another witness and one who would be admitted to oath.

Weigand bored holes into four of the discs and threw them, jesting kindly, into the children's apron. The others he kept. "He has pronounced his own condemnation," Toni thought as with trembling fingers she mended an old toy to fit the new wheels.

Nothing remained but to grind the proper dose with cinnamon, to sweeten it—according to instructions—and spice a rice-pudding therewith.

But fate which, in this delicate matter, had been hostile to her from the beginning, ordained it otherwise.

For that very evening came the apothecary, not, as a rule, a timid person. He was pale and showed Weigand the fruits. He had, by the merest hair-breadth, prevented his little girl Marie from nibbling one of them.

The rest followed as a matter of course. The new wheels were taken from the doll-carriage, all fragments were carefully sought out and all the discs were given to the apothecary who locked them into his safe.

"The red-headed girl must be sacrificed after all," Toni thought.

She planned and schemed, but she could think of no way by which the waitress could be saved from that destruction which hung over her.

There was no room for further hestiation. The path had to be trodden to its goal. Whether she left corpses on the way-side, whether she herself broke down dead at the goal—it did not matter. That plan of her life which rivetted her fate to her beloved's forever demanded that she proceed.

The old physician came hurrying to the inn next morning. He was utterly confounded by the scarcely escaped horrors.

"You really look," he said to Toni, "as if you had swallowed some of the stuff, too."

"Oh, I suppose my fate will overtake me in the end," she answered with a weary smile. "I feel it in my bones: there will be some misfortune in our house."

"For heaven's sake!" he cried, "Put that red-headed beast into the street."

"It isn't she! I'll take my oath on that," she said eagerly and thought that she had done a wonderfully clever thing.

She waited in suspense, fearing that the authorities would take a closer look at this last incident. She was equipped for any search—even one that might penetrate to her own bed-room. For she had put false bottoms into the little medicine-boxes. Beneath these she kept the arsenic. On top lay harmless magnesia. The boxes themselves stood on her toilet-table, exposed to all eyes and hence withdrawn from all suspicion.

She waited till evening, but nobody came. And yet the connection between this incident and the former one seemed easy enough to establish. However that might be, she assigned the final deed to the very next day. And why wait? An end had to be made of this torture of hesitation which, at every new scruple, seemed to freeze her very heart's blood. Furthermore the finding of the "crow's eyes" would be of use in leading justice astray.

To-morrow, then . . . to-morrow. . . .

Weigand had gone to bed early. But Toni sat behind the door of the public room and, through a slit of the door, listened to every movement of the waitress. She had kept near her all evening. She scarcely knew why. But a strange, dull hope would not die in her—a hope that something might happen whereby her unsuspecting victim and herself might both be saved.

The clock struck one. The public rooms were all but empty. Only a few young clerks remained. These were half-drunk and made rough advances to the waitress.

She resisted half-serious, half-jesting.

"You go out and cool yourselves in the night-air. I don't care about such fellows as you."

"I suppose you want only counts and barons," one of them taunted her. "I suppose you wouldn't even think the county-counsellor good enough!"

"That's my affair," she answered, "as to who is good enough for me. I have my choice. I can get any man I want."

They laughed at her and she flew into a rage.

"If you weren't such a beggarly crew and had anything to bet, I'd wager you any money that I'd seduce any man I want in a week. In a week, do I say? In three days! Just name the man."

Antonie quivered sharply and then sank with

closed eyes, against the back of her chair. A
dream of infinite bliss stole through her being.
Was there salvation for her in this world? Could
this coarse creature accomplish that in which
beauty and refinement had failed?

Could she be saved from becoming a mur-
deress? Would it be granted her to remain human, with a human soul and a human face?

But this was no time for tears or weakening.

With iron energy she summoned all her
strength and quietude and wisdom. The moment was a decisive one.

When the last guests had gone and all servants, too, had gone to their rest, she called the
waitress, with some jesting reproach, into her
room.

A long whispered conversation followed. At
its end the woman declared that the matter was
child's play to her.

And did not suspect that by this game she was
saving her life.

VII.

In hesitant incredulity Antonie awaited the things that were to come.

On the first day a staggering thing happened. The red-headed woman, scolding at the top of her voice, threw down a beer-glass at her master's feet, upon which he immediately gave her notice.

Toni's newly-awakened hope sank. The woman had boasted. And what was worse than all: if the final deed could be accomplished, her compact with the waitress would damn her. The woman would of course use this weapon ruthlessly. The affair had never stood so badly.

But that evening she breathed again. For Weigand declared that the waitress seemed to have her good qualities too and her heart-felt prayers had persuaded him to keep her.

For several days nothing of significance took place except that Weigand, whenever he mentioned the waitress, peered curiously aside. And this fact Toni interpreted in a favorable light.

Almost a week passed. Then, one day, the waitress approached Toni at an unwonted hour.

"If you'll just peep into my room this afternoon. . . ."

Toni followed directions. . . . The poor substitute crept down the stairs—caught and powerless. He followed his wife who knelt sobbing beside their bed. She was not to be comforted, nor to be moved. She repulsed him and wept and wept.

Weigand had never dreamed that he was so passionately loved. The more violent was the anger of the deceived wife. . . . She demanded divorce, instant divorce. . . .

He begged and besought and adjured. In vain.

Next he enlisted the sympathy of his father-in-law who had taken no great interest in the business during these years, but was content if the money he had invested in it paid the necessary six per cent. promptly.

The old man came immediately and made a scene with his recalcitrant daughter. . . . There was the splendid business and the heavy investment! She was not to think that he would give her one extra penny. He would simply withdraw his capital and let her and the child starve.

Toni did not even deign to reply.

The suit progressed rapidly. The unequivocal testimony of the waitress rendered any protest nugatory.

Three months later Toni put her possessions

on a train, took her child, whom the deserted father followed with an inarticulate moan, and travelled to Koenigsberg where she rented a small flat in order to await in quiet the reunion with her beloved.

The latter was trying to work up a practice in a village close to the Russian border. He wrote that things were going slowly and that, hence, he must be at his post night and day. So soon as he had the slightest financial certainty for his wife and child, he would come for them.

And so she awaited the coming of her life's happiness. She had little to do, and passed many happy hours in imagining how he would rush in— by yonder passage—through this very door—tall and slender and impassioned and press her to his wildly throbbing heart. And ever again, though she knew it to be a foolish dream, did she see the blue white golden scarf upon his chest and the blue and gold cap upon his blond curls.

Lonely widows—even those of the divorced variety—find friends and ready sympathy in the land of good hearts. But Antonie avoided everyone who sought her society. Under the ban of her great secret purpose she had ceased to regard men and women except as they could be turned into the instruments of her will. And her use for them was over. As for their merely human character and experience—Toni saw through these at once. And it all seemed to her futile and trivial in the fierce reflection of those infernal fires through which she had had to pass.

Adorned like a bride and waiting—thus she lived quietly and modestly on the means which her divorced husband—in order to keep his own head above water—managed to squeeze out of the business.

Suddenly her father died. People said that his death was due to unconquerable rage over her folly. . . .

She buried him, bearing herself all the while with blameless filial piety and then awoke to the fact that she was rich.

She wrote to her beloved: "Don't worry another day. We are in a position to choose the kind of life that pleases us."

He wired back: "Expect me to-morrow."

Full of delight and anxiety she ran to the mirror and discovered for the thousandth time, that she was beautiful again. The results of poisoning had disappeared, crime and degradation had burned no marks into her face. She stood there—a ruler of life. Her whole being seemed sure of itself, kindly, open. Only the wild glance might, at times, betray the fact that there was much to conceal.

She kept wakeful throughout the night, as she

had done through many another. Plan after plan passed through her busy brain. It was with an effort that she realised the passing of such grim necessities.

VIII.

A BUNCH of crysanthemums stood on the table, asters in vases on dresser and chiffonier—colourful and scentless.

Antonie wore a dress of black lace that had been made by the best dress-maker in the city for this occasion. In festive array she desired to meet her beloved and yet not utterly discard the garb of filial grief. But she had dressed the child in white, with white silk stockings and sky-blue ribands. It was to meet its father like the incarnate spirit of approaching happiness.

From the kitchen came the odours of the choicest autumn dishes—roast duck with apples and a grape-cake, such as she alone knew how to prepare. Two bottles of precious Rhine wine stood in the cool without the window. She did not want to welcome him with champagne. The memories of its subtle prickling, and of much else connected therewith, nauseated her.

If he left his village at six in the morning he must arrive at noon.

And she waited even as she had waited seven years. This morning seven hours had been left,

133

there were scarcely seven minutes now. And then—the door-bell rang.

"That is the new uncle," she said to Amanda who was handling her finery, flattered and astonished, and she wondered to note her brain grow suddenly so cool and clear.

A gentleman entered. A strange gentleman. Wholly strange. Had she met him on the street she would not have known him.

He had grown old—forty, fifty, an hundred years. Yet his real age could not be over twenty-eight! . . . .

He had grown fat. He carried a little paunch about with him, round and comfortable. And the honourable scars gleamed in round red cheeks. His eyes seemed small and receding. . . .

And when he said: "Here I am at last," it was no longer the old voice, clear and a little resonant, which had echoed and re-echoed in her spiritual ear. He gurgled as though he had swallowed dumplings.

But when he took her hand and smiled, something slipt into his face—something affectionate and quiet, empty and without guile or suspicion.

Where was she accustomed to this smile? To be sure; in Amanda. An indubitable inheritance.

And for the sake of this empty smile an affectionate feeling for this stranger came into her heart.

She helped him take off his overcoat. He wore a pair of great, red-lined rubber goloshes, typical of the country doctor. He took these off carefully and placed them with their toes toward the wall.

"He has grown too pedantic," she thought.

Then all three entered the room. When Toni saw him in the light of day she missed the blue white golden scarf at once. But it would have looked comical over his rounded paunch. And yet its absence disillusioned her. It seemed to her as if her friend had doffed the halo for whose sake she had served him and looked up to him so long.

As for him, he regarded her with unconcealed admiration.

"Well, well, one can be proud of you!" he said, sighing deeply, and it almost seemed as if with this sigh a long and heavy burden lifted itself from his soul.

"He was afraid he might have to be ashamed of me," she thought rebelliously. As if to protect herself she pushed the little girl between them.

"Here is Amanda," she said, and added with a bitter smile: "Perhaps you remember."

But he didn't even suspect the nature of that which she wanted to make him feel.

"Oh, I've brought something for you, little

one!" he cried with the delight of one who recalls an important matter in time. With measured step he trotted back into the hall and brought out a flat paste-board box tied with pink ribands. He opened it very carefully and revealed a layer of chocolate-creams wrapped in tin-foil and offered one to Amanda.

And this action seemed to him, obviously, to satisfy all requirements in regard to his preliminary relations to the child.

Antonie felt the approach of a head-ache such as she had now and then ever since the arsenic poisoning.

"You are probably hungry, dear Robert," she said.

He wouldn't deny that. "If one is on one's legs from four o'clock in the morning on, you know, and has nothing in one's stomach but a couple of little sausages, you know!"

He said all that with the same cheerfulness that seemed to come to him as a matter of course and yet did not succeed in wholly hiding an inner diffidence.

They sat down at the table and Antonie, taking pleasure in seeing to his comfort, forgot for a moment the foolish ache that tugged at her body and at her soul.

The wine made him talkative. He related everything that interested him—his professional

trips across country, the confinements that sometimes came so close together that he had to spend
twenty-four hours in his buggy. Then he told
of the tricks by which people whose lives he had
just saved sought to cheat him out of his modest
fees. And he told also of the comfortable card-
parties with the judge and the village priest.
And how funny it was when the inn-keeper's
tame starling promenaded on the cards. . . .

Every word told of cheerful well-being and
unambitious contentment.

"He doesn't think of our common future," a
torturing suspicion whispered to her.

But he did.

"I should like to have you try, first of all,
Toni, to live there. It isn't easy. But we can
both stand a good deal, thank God, and if
we don't like it in the end, why, we can move
away."

And he said that so simply and sincerely that
her suspicion vanished.

And with this returning certitude there returned, too, the ambition which she had always
nurtured for him.

"How would it be if we moved to Berlin, or
somewhere where there is a university?"

"And maybe aim at a professorship?" he cried
with cheerful irony. "No, Tonichen, all your
money can't persuade me to that. I crammed

enough in that damned medical school. I've got
my income and that's good enough for me."

A feeling of disgust came over her. She
seemed to perceive the stuffy odour of unventi-
lated rooms and of decaying water in which
flowers had stood.

"That is what I suffered for," involuntarily the
thought came, *"that!"*

After dinner when Amanda was sleeping off
the effects of the little sip of wine which she had
taken when they let her clink glasses with them,
they sat opposite each other beside the geraniums
of the window-box and fell silent. He blew
clouds of smoke from his cigar into the air
and seemed not disinclined to indulge in a nap,
too.

Leaning back in her wicker chair she observed
him uninterruptedly. At one moment it seemed
to her as though she caught an intoxicating remnant of the slim, pallid lad to whom she had
given her love. And then again came the cor-
roding doubt: "Was it for him, for him. . . ."
And then a great fear oppressed her heart, because this man seemed to live in a world which
she could not reach in a whole life's pilgrimage.
Walls had arisen between them, doors had been
bolted—doors that rose from the depths of the
earth to the heights of heaven. . . . As he
sat there, surrounded by the blue smoke of his

cigar, he seemed more and more to recede into immeasurable distances. . . .

Then, suddenly, as if an inspiration had come to him, he pulled himself together, and his face became serious, almost solemn. He laid the cigar down on the window-box and pulled out of his inner pocket a bundle of yellow sheets of paper and blue note-books.

"I should have done this a long time ago," he said, "because we've been free to correspond with each other. But I put it off to our first meeting."

"Done what?" she asked, seized by an uncomfortable curiosity.

"Why, render an accounting."

"An accounting?"

"But dear Toni, surely you don't think me either ungrateful or dishonourable. For seven years I have accepted one benefaction after another from you. . . . That was a very painful situation for me, dear child, and I scarcely believe that the circumstances, had they been known, would ever have been countenanced by a court of honour."

"Ah, yes," she said slowly. "I confess I never thought of *that* consideration. . . ."

"But I did all the more, for that very reason. And only the consciousness that I would some day be able to pay you the last penny of my debt sustained me in my consciousness as a decent fellow."

"Ah, well, if that's the case, go ahead!" she said, suppressing the bitter sarcasm that she felt.

First came the receipts: The proceeds of the stolen jewels began the long series. Then followed the savings in fares, food and drink and the furniture rebates. Next came the presents of the county-counsellor, the profits of the champagne debauches during which she had flung shame and honour under the feet of the drinking men. She was spared nothing, but heard again of sums gained by petty thefts from the till, small profits made in the buying of milk and eggs. It was a long story of suspense and longing, an inextricable web of falsification and trickery, of terror and lying without end. The memory of no guilt and no torture was spared her.

Then he took up the account of his expenditures. He sat there, eagerly handling the papers, now frowning heavily when he could not at once balance some small sum, now stiffening his double chin in satisfied self-righteousness as he explained some new way of saving that had occurred to him. . . . Again and again, to the point of weariness, he reiterated solemnly: "You see, I'm an honest man."

And always when he said that, a weary irony

prompted her to reply: "Ah, what that honesty has cost me." . . . But she held her peace.

And again she wanted to cry out: "Let be! A woman like myself doesn't care for these two-penny decencies." But she saw how deep an inner necessity it was to him to stand before her in this conventional spotlessness. And so she didn't rob him of his child-like joy.

At last he made an end and spread out the little blue books before her—there was one for each year. "Here," he said proudly, "you can go over it yourself. It's exact."

"It had better be!" she cried with a jesting threat and put the little books under a flower-pot.

A prankish mood came upon her now which she couldn't resist.

"Now that this important business is at an end," she said, "there is still another matter about which I must have some certainty."

"What is that?" he said, listening intensely.

"Have you been faithful to me in all this time?"

He became greatly confused. The scars on his left cheek glowed like thick, red cords.

"Perhaps he's got a betrothed somewhere," she thought with a kind of woeful anger, "whom he's going to throw over now."

But it wasn't that. Not at all.

"Well," he said, "there's no help for it. I'll confess. And anyhow, *you've* even been married in the meantime."

"I would find it difficult to deny that," she said.

And then everything came to light. During the early days in Berlin he had been very intimate with a waitress. Then, when he was an assistant in the surgical clinic, there had been a sister who even wanted to be married. "But I made short work of that proposition," he explained with quiet decision. And as for the Lithuanian servant girl whom he had in the house now, why, of course he would dismiss her next morning, so that the house could be thoroughly aired before she moved in.

This was the moment in which a desire came upon her—half-ironic, half-compassionate—to throw her arms about him and say: "You silly boy!"

But she did not yield and in the next moment the impulse was gone. Only an annoyed envy remained. He dared to confess everything to her—everything. What if she did the same? If he were to leave her in horrified silence, what would it matter? She would have freed her soul. Or perhaps he would flare up in grateful love? It was madness to expect it. No power of heaven or earth could burst open the doors or demolish the walls that towered between them for all eternity.

A vast irony engulfed her. She could not rest her soul upon this pigmy. She felt revengeful rather toward him—revengeful, because he could sit there opposite her so capable and faithful, so truthful and decent, so utterly unlike the companion whom she needed.

Toward twilight he grew restless. He wanted to slip over to his mother for a moment and then, for another moment, he wanted to drop in at the fraternity inn. He had to leave at eight.

"It would be better if you remained until to-morrow," she said with an emphasis that gave him pause.

"Why?"

"If you don't feel that. . . ."

She shrugged her shoulders.

It wasn't to be done, he assured her, with the best will in the world. There was an investigation in which he had to help the county-physician. A small farmer had died suddenly of what did not seem an entirely natural death. "I suppose," he continued, "one of those love philtres was used with which superfluous people are put under ground there. It's horrible that a decent person has to live among such creatures. If you don't care to do it, I can hardly blame you."

She had grown pale and smiled weakly. She restrained him no longer.

"I'll be back in a week," he said, slipping on his goloshes, "and then we can announce the engagement."

She nodded several times but made no reply.

The door was opened and he leaned toward her. Calmly she touched his lips with hers.

"You might have the announcement cards printed," he called cheerfully from the stairs.

Then he disappeared. . . .

"Is the new uncle gone?" Amanda asked. She was sitting in her little room, busy with her lessons. He had forgotten her.

The mother nodded.

"Will he come back soon?"

Antonie shook her head.

"I scarcely think so," she answered.

That night she broke the purpose of her life, the purpose that had become interwoven with a thousand others, and when the morning came she wrote a letter of farewell to the beloved of her youth.

SONG OF DEATH

THE SONG OF DEATH

WITH faint and quivering beats the clock of the hotel announced the hour to the promenaders on the beach.

"It is time to eat, Nathaniel," said a slender, yet well-filled-out young woman, who held a book between her fingers, to a formless bundle, huddled in many shawls, by her side. Painfully the bundle unfolded itself, stretched and grew gradually into the form of a man—hollow chested, thin legged, narrow shouldered, attired in flopping garments, such as one sees by the thousands on the coasts of the Riviera in winter.

The midday glow of the sun burned down upon the yellowish gray wall of cliff into which the promenade of Nervi is hewn, and which slopes down to the sea in a zigzag of towering bowlders.

Upon the blue mirror of the sea sparkled a silvery meshwork of sunbeams. So vast a fullness of light flooded the landscape that even the black cypress trees which stood, straight and tall, beyond the garden walls, seemed to glitter with a radiance of their own.

The tide was silent. Only the waters of the imprisoned springs that poured, covered with iridescent bubbles, into the hollows between the rocks, gurgled and sighed wearily.

The breakfast bell brought a new pulsation of life to the huddled figures on the beach.

"He who eats is cured," is the motto of the weary creatures whose arms are often too weak to carry their forks to their mouths. But he who comes to this land of eternal summer merely to ease and rest his soul, trembles with hunger in the devouring sweetness of the air and can scarcely await the hour of food.

With a gentle compulsion the young woman pushed the thin, wrinkled hand of the invalid under her arm and led him carefully through a cool and narrow road, which runs up to the town between high garden walls and through which a treacherous draught blows even on the sunniest days.

"Are you sure your mouth is covered?" she asked, adapting her springy gait with difficulty to the dragging steps of her companion.

An inarticulate murmur behind the heavy shawl was his only answer.

She stretched her throat a little—a round, white, firm throat, with two little folds that lay rosy in the rounded flesh. Closing her eyes, she inhaled passionately the aromatic perfumes

of the neighbouring gardens. It was a strange
mixture of odours, like that which is wafted
from the herb chamber of an apothecary. A
wandering sunbeam glided over the firm, short
curve of her cheek, which was of almost milky
whiteness, save for the faint redness of those
veins which sleepless nights bring out upon the
pallid faces of full-blooded blondes.

A laughing group of people went swiftly by
—white-breeched Englishmen and their ladies.
The feather boas, whose ends fluttered in the
wind, curled tenderly about slender throats, and
on the reddish heads bobbed little round hats,
smooth and shining as the tall head-gear of a
German postillion.

The young woman cast a wistful glance after
those happy folk, and pressed more firmly the
arm of her suffering husband.

Other groups followed. It was not difficult
to overtake this pair.

"We'll be the last, Mary," Nathaniel murmured, with the invalid's ready reproach.

But the young woman did not hear. She
listened to a soft chatting, which, carried along
between the sounding-boards of these high walls,
was clearly audible. The conversation was
conducted in French, and she had to summon
her whole stock of knowledge in order not to lose
the full sense of what was said.

"I hope, Madame, that your uncle is not seriously ill?"

"Not at all, sir. But he likes his comfort. And since walking bores him, he prefers to pass his days in an armchair. And it's my function to entertain him." An arch, pouting *voila* closed the explanation.

Next came a little pause. Then the male voice asked:

"And are you never free, Madame?"

"Almost never."

"And may I never again hope for the happiness of meeting you on the beach?"

"But surely you may!"

"Mille remerciments, Madame."

A strangely soft restrained tone echoed in this simple word of thanks. Secret desires murmured in it and unexpressed confessions.

Mary, although she did not look as though she were experienced in flirtation or advances, made a brief, timid gesture. Then, as though discovered and ashamed, she remained very still.

Those two then. . .   That's who it was. . .

And they had really made each others' acquaintance!

She was a delicately made and elegant Frenchwoman. Her bodice was cut in a strangely slender way, which made her seem to glide along like a bird. Or was it her walk that caused the phenomenon? Or the exquisite arching of her shoulders? Who could tell? . . . She did not take her meals at the common table, but in a corner of the dining-hall in company of an old gouty gentleman with white stubbles on his chin and red-lidded eyes. When she entered the hall she let a smiling glance glide along the table, but without looking at or saluting any one. She scarcely touched the dishes—at least from the point of view of Mary's sturdy appetite—but even before the soup was served she nibbled at the dates meant for dessert, and then the bracelets upon her incredibly delicate wrists made a strange, fairy music. She wore a wedding ring. But it had always been open to doubt whether the old gentleman was her husband. For her demeanour toward him was that of a spoiled but sedulously watched child.

And he—he sat opposite Mary at table. He was a very dark young man, with black, melancholy eyes—Italian eyes, one called them in her Pomeranian home land. He had remarkably white, narrow hands, and a small, curly beard, which was clipped so close along the cheeks that the skin itself seemed to have a bluish shimmer. He had never spoken to Mary, presumably because he knew no German, but now and then he would let his eyes rest upon her with a certain smiling emotion which seemed to her to be very blameworthy and which filled her with confusion. Thus, however, it had come to pass that, whenever she got ready to go to table her thoughts were busy with him, and it was not rare for her to ask herself at the opening of the door to the dining-hall: "I wonder whether he's here or will come later?"

For several days there had been noticeable in this young man an inclination to gaze over his left shoulder to the side table at which the young Frenchwoman sat. And several times this glance had met an answering one, however fleeting. And more than that! She could be seen observing him with smiling consideration as, between the fish and the roast, she pushed one grape after another between her lips. He was, of course, not cognisant of all that, but Mary knew of it and was surprised and slightly shocked.

And they had really made each others' acquaintance!

And now they were both silent, thinking, obviously, that they had but just come within hearing distance.

Then they hurried past the slowly creeping couple. The lady looked downward, kicking pebbles; the gentleman bowed. It was done seriously, discreetly, as befits a mere neighbour at table.

Mary blushed. That happened often, far too often. And she was ashamed. Thus it happened that she often blushed from fear of blushing.

The gentleman saw it and did not smile. She thanked him for it in her heart, and blushed all the redder, for he *might* have smiled.

"We'll have to eat the omelettes cold again," the invalid mumbled into his shawls.

This time she understood him.

"Then we'll order fresh ones."

"Oh," he said reproachfully, "you haven't the courage. You're always afraid of the waiters."

She looked up at him with a melancholy smile.

It was true. She was afraid of the waiters. That could not be denied. Her necessary dealings with these dark and shiny-haired gentlemen in evening clothes were a constant source of fear and annoyance. They scarcely gave themselves the trouble to understand her bad French and her worse Italian. And when they dared to smile . . . !

But his concern had been needless. The breakfast did not consist of omelettes, but of macaroni boiled in water and mixed with long strings of cheese. He was forbidden to eat this dish.

Mary mixed his daily drink, milk with brandy, and was happy to see the eagerness with which he absorbed the life-giving fumes.

The dark gentleman was already in his seat opposite her, and every now and then the glance of his velvety eyes glided over her. She was more keenly conscious of this glance than ever, and dared less than ever to meet it. A strange feeling, half delight and half resentment, overcame her. And yet she had no cause to complain that his attention passed the boundary of rigid seemliness.

She stroked her heavy tresses of reddish blonde hair, which curved madonna-like over her temples. They had not been crimped or curled, but were simple and smooth, as befits the wife of a North German clergyman. She would have liked to moisten with her lips the fingers with which she stroked them. This was the only art of the toilet which she knew. But that would have been improper at table.

He wore a yellow silk shirt with a pattern of riding crops. A bunch of violets stuck in his button-hole. Its fragrance floated across the table.

Now the young Frenchwoman entered the hall too. Very carefully she pressed her old uncle's arm, and talked to him in a stream of charming chatter.

The dark gentleman quivered. He compressed his lips but did not turn around. Neither did the lady take any notice of him. She rolled bread pellets with her nervous fingers, played with her bracelets and let the dishes go by untouched.

The long coat of cream silk, which she had put on, increased the tall flexibility of her form. A being woven of sunlight and morning dew, unapproachable in her serene distinction—thus she appeared to Mary, whose hands had been reddened by early toil, and whose breadth of shoulder was only surpassed by her simplicity of heart.

When the roast came Nathaniel revived slightly. He suffered her to fasten the shawl about his shoulders, and rewarded her with a contented smile. It was her sister Anna's opinion that at such moments he resembled the Saviour. The eyes in their blue hollows gleamed with a ghostly light, a faint rosiness shone upon his cheek-bones, and even the blonde beard on the sunken cheeks took on a certain glow.

Grateful for the smile, she pressed his arm. She was satisfied with so little.

Breakfast was over. The gentleman opposite made his silent bow and arose.

"Will he salute her?" Mary asked herself with some inner timidity.

No. He withdrew without glancing at the corner table.

"Perhaps they have fallen out again," Mary said to herself.

The lady looked after him. A gentle smile played about the corners of her mouth—a superior, almost an ironical smile. Then, her eyes still turned to the door, she leaned across toward the old gentleman in eager questioning.

"She doesn't care for him," Mary reasoned, with a slight feeling of satisfaction. It was as though some one had returned to her what she had deemed lost.

He had been gone long, but his violets had left their fragrance.

Mary went up to her room to get a warmer shawl for Nathaniel. As she came out again, she saw in the dim hall the radiant figure of the French lady come toward her and open the door to the left of her own room.

"So we are neighbours," Mary thought, and felt flattered by the proximity. She would have liked to salute her, but she did not dare.

Then she accompanied Nathaniel down to the promenade on the beach. The hours dragged by.

He did not like to have his brooding meditation interrupted by questions or anecdotes. These hours were dedicated to getting well. Every breath here cost money and must be utilised to the utmost. Here breathing was religion, and falling ill a sin.

Mary looked dreamily out upon the sea, to

which the afternoon sun now lent a deeper blue.
Light wreaths of foam eddied about the stones.
In wide semicircles the great and shadowy arms
of the mountains embraced the sea. From
the far horizon, in regions of the upper air,
came from time to time an argent gleam. For
there the sun was reflected by unseen fields of
snow.

There lay the Alps, and beyond them, deep
buried in fog and winter, lay their home land.

Thither Mary's thoughts wandered. They
wandered to a sharp-gabled little house, groan-
ing under great weights of snow, by the strand
of a frozen stream. The house was so deeply
hidden in bushes that the depending boughs froze
fast in the icy river and were not liberated till
the tardy coming of spring.

And a hundred paces from it stood the white
church and the comfortable parsonage. But
what did she care for the parsonage, even though
she had grown to womanhood in it and was now
its mistress?

That little cottage—the widow's house, as the
country folk called it—that little cottage held
everything that was dear to her at home. There
sat by the green tile oven—and oh, how she
missed it here, despite the palms and the goodly
sun—her aged mother, the former pastor's
widow, and her three older sisters, dear and

blonde and thin and almost faded. There they sat, worlds away, needy and laborious, and living but in each others' love. Four years had passed since the father had been carried to the God's acre and they had had to leave the parsonage.

That had marked the end of their happiness and their youth. They could not move to the city, for they had no private means, and the gifts of the poor congregation, a dwelling, wood and other donations, could not be exchanged for money. And so they had to stay there quietly and see their lives wither.

The candidate of theology, Nathaniel Pogge, equipped with mighty recommendations, came to deliver his trial sermon.

As he ascended the pulpit, long and frail, flat-chested and narrow shouldered, she saw him for the first time. His emaciated, freckled hand which held the hymn book, trembled with a kind of fever. But his blue eyes shone with the fires of God. To be sure, his voice sounded hollow and hoarse, and often he had to struggle for breath in the middle of a sentence. But what he said was wise and austere, and found favour in the eyes of his congregation.

His mother moved with him into the parsonage. She was a small, fussy lady, energetic and very business-like, who complained of what she called previous mismanagement and seemed to avoid friendly relations.

But her son found his way to the widow's house for all that. He found it oftener and oftener, and the only matter of uncertainty was as to which of the four sisters had impressed him.

She would never have dreamed that his eye had fallen upon her, the youngest. But a refusal was not to be thought of. It was rather her duty to kiss his hands in gratitude for taking her off her mother's shoulders and liberating her from a hopeless situation. Certainly she would not have grudged her happiness to one of her sisters; if it could be called happiness to be subject to a suspicious mother-in-law and the nurse of a valetudinarian. But she tried to think it happiness. And, after all, there was the widow's house, to which one could slip over to laugh or to weep one's fill, as the mood of the hour dictated. Either would have been frowned upon at home.

And of course she loved him.

Assuredly. How should she not have loved him? Had she not sworn to do so at the altar? And then his condition grew worse from day to day and needed her love all the more.

It happened ever oftener that she had to get up at night to heat his moss tea; and ever more breathlessly he cowered in the sacristy after his

weekly sermon. And that lasted until the hem-
orrhage came, which made the trip south impera-
tive.

Ah, and with what grave anxieties had this
trip been undertaken! A substitute had to be
procured. Their clothes and fares swallowed the
salary of many months. They had to pay four-
teen francs board a day, not to speak of the extra expenses for brandy, milk, fires and drugs.
Nor was this counting the physician who came
daily. It was a desperate situation.

But he recovered. At least it was unthinkable
that he shouldn't. What object else would these
sacrifices have had?

He recovered. The sun and sea and air cured
him; or, at least, her love cured him. And this
love, which Heaven had sent her as her highest
duty, surrounded him like a soft, warm garment,
exquisitely flexible to the movement of every
limb, not hindering, but yielding to the slightest
impulse of movement; forming a protection
against the rough winds of the world, surer than
a wall of stone or a cloak of fire.

The sun sank down toward the sea. His light
assumed a yellow, metallic hue, hard and wounding, before it changed and softened into violet
and purple shades. The group of pines on the
beach seemed drenched in a sulphurous light and
the clarity of their outlines hurt the eye. Like

a heavy and compact mass, ready to hurtle down, the foliage of the gardens bent over the crumbling walls. From the mountains came a gusty wind that announced the approaching fall of night.

The sick man shivered. Mary was about to suggest their going home, when she perceived the form of a man that had intruded between her and the sinking sun and that was surrounded by a yellow radiance. She recognised the dark gentleman.

A feeling of restlessness overcame her, but she could not turn her eyes from him. Always, when he was near, a strange presentiment came to her —a dreamy knowledge of an unknown land. This impression varied in clearness. To-night she was fully conscious of it.

What she felt was difficult to put into words. She seemed almost to be afraid of him. And yet that was impossible, for what was he to her? She wasn't even interested in him. Surely not. His eyes, his violet fragrance, the flexible elegance of his movements—these things merely aroused in her a faint curiosity. Strictly speaking, he wasn't even a sympathetic personality, and had her sister Lizzie, who had a gift for satire, been here, they would probably have made fun of him. The anxious unquiet which he inspired must have some other source.

Here in the south everything was so different
—richer, more colourful, more vivid than at
home. The sun, the sea, houses, flowers, faces—
upon them all lay more impassioned hues. Behind all that there must be a secret hitherto un-
revealed to her.

She felt this secret everywhere. It lay in
the heavy fragrance of the trees, in the soft
swinging of the palm leaves, in the multitudin-
ous burgeoning and bloom about her. It lay in
the long-drawn music of the men's voices, in
the caressing laughter of the women. It lay in
the flaming blushes that, even at table, mantled
her face; in the delicious languor that pervaded
her limbs and seemed to creep into the innermost marrow of her bones.

But this secret which she felt, scented and absorbed with every organ of her being, but which
was nowhere to be grasped, looked upon or recognised—this secret was in some subtle way connected with the man who stood there, irradiated,
upon the edge of the cliff, and gazed upon the
ancient tower which stood, unreal as a piece of
stage scenery, upon the path.

Now he observed her.

For a moment it seemed as though he were
about to approach to address her. In his character of a neighbour at table he might well
have ventured to do so. But the hasty gesture

with which she turned to her sick husband forbade it.

"That would be the last inconvenience," Mary thought, "to make acquaintances."

But as she was going home with her husband, she surprised herself in speculation as to how she might have answered his words.

"My French will go far enough," she thought. "At need I might have risked it."

The following day brought a sudden lapse in her husband's recovery.

"That happens often," said the physician, a bony consumptive with the manners of a man of the world and an equipment in that inexpensive courtesy which doctors are wont to assume in hopeless and poorly paying cases.

To listen to him one would think that pulmonary consumption ended in invariable improvement.

"And if something happens during the night?" Mary asked anxiously.

"Then just wait quietly until morning," the doctor said with the firm decision of a man who doesn't like to have his sleep disturbed.

Nathaniel had to stay in bed and Mary was forced to request the waiters to bring meals up to their room.

Thus passed several days, during which she scarcely left the sick-bed of her husband. And when she wasn't writing home, or reading to him from the hymn book, or cooking some easing draught upon the spirit lamp, she gazed dreamily out of the window.

She had not seen her beautiful neighbour again. With all the more attention she sought to catch any sound, any word that might give her a glimpse into the radiant Paradise of that other life.

A soft singing ushered in the day. Then followed a laughing chatter with the little maid, accompanied by the rattle of heated curling-irons and splashing of bath sponges. Occasionally, too, there was a little dispute on the subject of ribands or curls or such things. Mary's French, which was derived from the *Histoire de Charles douze,* the *Aventures de Télémaque* and other lofty books, found an end when it came to these discussions.

About half-past ten the lady slipped from her room. Then one could hear her tap at her uncle's door, or call a laughing good-morning to him from the hall.

From now on the maid reigned supreme in the room. She straightened it, sang, rattled the curling-irons even longer than for her mistress, tripped up and down, probably in front of the mirror, and received the kindly attentions of several waiters.

From noon on everything was silent and remained silent until dusk. Then the lady returned. The little songs she sang were of the very kind that one might well sing if, with full heart, one gazes out upon the sea, while the orange-blossoms are fragrant and the boughs of the eucalyptus rustle. They proved to Mary that in that sunny creature, as in herself, there dwelt that gentle, virginal yearning that had always been to her a source of dreamy happiness.

At half-past five o'clock the maid knocked at the door. Then began giggling and whispering as of two school-girls. Again sounded the rattle of the curling-irons and the rustling of silken skirts. The fragrance of unknown perfumes and essences penetrated into Mary's room, and she absorbed it eagerly.

The dinner-bell rang and the room was left empty.

At ten o'clock there resounded a merry: *"Bonne nuit, mon oncle!"*

Angeline, the maid, received her mistress at the door and performed the necessary services more quietly than before. Then she went out, received by the waiters, who were on the stairs.

Then followed, in there, a brief evening prayer, carelessly and half poutingly gabbled as by a tired child.

At eleven the keyhole grew dark. And during the hours of Mary's heaviest service, there sounded within the peaceful drawing of uninterrupted breath.

This breathing was a consolation to her during the terrible, creeping hours, whose paralysing monotony was only interrupted by anxious crises in the patient's condition.

The breathing seemed to her a greeting from a pure and sisterly soul—a greeting from that dear land of joy where one can laugh by day and sing in the dusk and sleep by night.

Nathaniel loved the hymns for the dying.

He asserted that they filled him with true mirth. The more he could gibe at hell or hear the suffering of the last hours put to scorn, the more could he master a kind of grim humour. He, the shepherd of souls, felt it his duty to venture upon the valley of the shadow to which he had so often led the trembling candidate of death, with the boldness of a hero in battle.

This poor, timid soul, who had never been able to endure the angry barking of a dog, played with the terror of death like a bull-necked gladiator.

"Read me a song of death, but a strengthening one," he would say repeatedly during the day, but also at night, if he could not sleep. He needed it as a child needs its cradle song.

Often he was angry when in her confusion and blinded by unshed tears, she chose a wrong one. Like a literary connoisseur who rolls a Horatian ode or a Goethean lyric upon his tongue—even thus he enjoyed these sombre stanzas.

There was one: "I haste to my eternal home," in which the beyond was likened to a bridal chamber and to a "crystal sea of blessednesses." There was another: "Greatly rejoice now, O my soul," which would admit no redeeming feature about this earth, and was really a prayer for release. And there was one filled with the purest folly of Christendom: "In peace and joy I fare from hence." And this one promised a smiling sleep. But they were all overshadowed by that rejoicing song: "Thank God, the hour has come!" which, like a cry of victory, points proudly and almost sarcastically to the conquered miseries of the earth.

The Will to Live of the poor flesh intoxicated itself with these pious lies as with some hypnotic drug. But at the next moment it recoiled and gazed yearningly and eager eyed out into the sweet and sinful world, which didn't tally in the least with that description of it as a vale of tears, of which the hymns were so full.

Mary read obediently what he demanded. Close to her face she held the narrow hymn-book, fighting down her sobs. For he did not think of the tortures he prepared for his anxiously hoping wife.

Why did he thirst for death since he knew that he *must* not die?

Not yet. Ah, not yet! Now that suddenly a whole, long, unlived life lay between them—a life they had never even suspected.

She could not name it, this new, rich life, but she felt it approaching, day by day. It breathed its fragrant breath into her face and poured an exquisite bridal warmth into her veins.

It was on the fourth day of his imprisonment in his room. The physician had promised him permission to go out on the morrow.

His recovery was clear.

She sat at the window and inhaled with quivering nostrils the sharp fragrance of the burning pine cones that floated to her in bluish waves.

The sun was about to set. An unknown bird sat, far below, in the orange grove and, as if drunk with light and fragrance, chirped sleepily and ended with a fluting tone.

Now that the great dread of the last few days was taken from her, that sweet languor the significance of which she could not guess came over her again.

Her neighbour had already come home. She opened her window and closed it, only to open it again. From time to time she sang a few brief tones, almost like the strange bird in the grove.

Then her door rattled and Angeline's voice cried out with jubilant laughter: *"Une lettre, Madame, une lettre!"*

"Une lettre—de qui?"

"De lui!"

Then a silence fell, a long silence.

Who was this "he?" Surely some one at home. It was the hour of the mail delivery.

But the voice of the maid soon brought enlightenment.

She had managed the affair cleverly. She had met him in the hall and saluted him so that he had found the courage to address her. And just now he had pressed the envelope, together with a twenty-franc piece, into her hand. He asserted that he had an important communication to make to her mistress, but had never found an opportunity to address himself to her in person.

"Tais-toi donc—on nous entend!"

And from now on nothing was to be heard but whispering and giggling.

Mary felt now a wave of hotness, started from her nape and overflowing her face.

Listening and with beating heart, she sat there.

What in all the world could he have written? For that it was he, she could no longer doubt.

Perhaps he had declared his love and begged for the gift of her hand.

A dull feeling of pain, the cause of which was dark to her, oppressed her heart.

And then she smiled—a smile of renouncement, although there was surely nothing here for her to renounce!

And anyhow—the thing was impossible. For she, to whom such an offer is made does not chat with a servant girl. Such an one flees into some lonely place, kneels down, and prays to God for enlightenment and grace in face of so important a step.

But indeed she did send the girl away, for the latter's slippers could be heard trailing along the hall.

Then was heard gentle, intoxicated laughter, full of restrained jubilation and arch triumph: *"O comme je suis heureuse! Comme je suis heureuse!"*

Mary felt her eyes grow moist. She felt glad and poignantly sad at the same time. She would have liked to kiss and bless the other woman, for now it was clear that he had come to claim her as his bride.

"If she doesn't pray, I will pray for her," she thought, and folded her hands. Then a voice sounded behind her, hollow as the roll of falling earth; rasping as coffin cords:

"Read me a song of death, Mary."

A shudder came over her. She jumped up.

And she who had hitherto taken up the hymn-book at his command without hesitation or complaint, fell down beside his bed and grasped his emaciated arm: "Have pity—I can't! I can't!"

Three days passed. The sick man preferred to stay in bed, although his recovery made enormous strides. Mary brewed his teas, gave him his drops, and read him his songs of death. That one attempt at rebellion had remained her only one.

She heard but little of her neighbour. It seemed that that letter had put an end to her talkative merriment. The happiness which she had so jubilantly confessed seemed to have been of brief duration.

And in those hours when Mary was free to pursue her dreams, she shared the other's yearning and fear. Probably the old uncle had made difficulties; had refused his consent, or even demanded the separation of the lovers.

Perhaps the dark gentleman had gone away. Who could tell?

"What strange eyes he had," she thought at times, and whenever she thought that, she shivered, for it seemed to her that his hot, veiled glance was still upon her.

"I wonder whether he is really a good man?" she asked herself. She would have liked to answer this question in the affirmative, but there was something that kept her from doing so. And there was another something in her that took but little note of that aspect, but only prayed that those two might be happy together, happy as she herself had never been, happy as—and here lay the secret.

It was a Sunday evening, the last one in January.

Nathaniel lay under the bed-clothes and breathed with difficulty. His fever was remarkably low, but he was badly smothered.

The lamp burned on the table—a reading lamp had been procured with difficulty and had been twice carried off in favour of wealthier guests. Toward the bed Mary had shaded the lamp with a piece of red blotting paper from her portfolio. A rosy shimmer poured out over the couch of the ill man, tinted the red covers more red, and caused a deceptive glow of health to appear on his cheek.

The flasks and vials on the table glittered with an equivocal friendliness, as though something of the demeanour of him who had prescribed their contents adhered to them.

Between them lay the narrow old hymnal and the gilt figures, "1795" shimmered in the middle of the worn and shabby covers.

The hour of retirement had come. The latest of the guests, returning from the reading room, had said good-night to each other in the hall. Angeline had been dismissed. Her giggles floated away into silence along the bannisters and the last of her adorers tiptoed by to turn out the lights.

From the next room there came no sound. She was surely asleep, although her breathing was inaudible.

Mary sat at the table. Her head was heavy and she stared into the luminous circle of the lamp. She needed sleep. Yet she was not sleepy. Every nerve in her body quivered with morbid energy.

A wish of the invalid called her to his side.

"The pillow has a lump," he said, and tried to turn over on his other side.

Ah, these pillows of sea-grass. She patted, she smoothed, she did her best, but his head found no repose.

"Here's another night full of the torment and terror of the flesh," he said with difficulty, mouthing each word.

"Do you want a drink?" she asked.

He shook his head.

"The stuff is bitter—but you see—this fear— there's the air and it fills everything—they say it's ten miles high—and a man like myself can't —get enough—you see I'm getting greedy."

The mild jest upon his lips was so unwonted that it frightened her.

"I'd like to ask you to open the window."

She opposed him.

"The night air," she urged; "the draught——"

But that upset him.

"If you can't do me so small a favour in my suffering——"

"Forgive me," she said, "it was only my anxiety for you——"

She got up and opened the French window that gave upon a narrow balcony.

The moonlight flooded the room.

Pressing her hands to her breast, she inhaled the first aromatic breath of the night air which cooled and caressed her hot face.

"Is it better so?" she asked, turning around.

He nodded. "It is better so."

Then she stepped out on the balcony. She could scarcely drink her fill of air and moonlight.

But she drew back, affrighted. What she had just seen was like an apparition.

On the neighbouring balcony stood, clad in white, flowing garments of lace, a woman's figure, and stared with wide open eyes into the moonlight.

It was she—her friend.

Softly Mary stepped out again and observed her, full of shy curiosity.

The moonlight shone full upon the delicate slim face, that seemed to shine with an inner radiance. The eye had a yearning glow. A smile, ecstatic and fearful at once, made the lips quiver, and the hands that grasped the iron railing pulsed as if in fear and expectation.

Mary heard her own heart begin to beat. A hot flush rose into her face?

What was all that? What did it mean?

Such a look, such a smile, she had never seen in her life. And yet both seemed infinitely familiar to her. Thus a woman must look who——

She had no time to complete the thought, for a fit of coughing recalled her to Nathaniel.

A motion of his hand directed her to close the window and the shutters. It would have been better never to have opened them. Better for her, too, perhaps.

Then she sat down next to him and held his head until the paroxysm was over.

He sank back, utterly exhausted. His hand groped for hers. With abstracted caresses she touched his weary fingers.

Her thoughts dwelt with that white picture without. That poignant feeling of happiness that she had almost lost during the past few days, arose in her with a hitherto unknown might.

And now the sick man began to speak.

"You have always been good to me, Mary,"

he said. "You have always had patience with me."

"Ah, don't speak so," she murmured.

"And I wish I could say as full of assurance as you could before the throne of God: 'Father, I have been true to the duty which you have allotted to me.'"

Her hand quivered in his. A feeling of revulsion smothered the gentleness of their mood. His words had struck her as a reproach.

Fulfillment of duty! That was the great law to which all human kind was subject for the sake of God. This law had joined her hand to his, had accompanied her into the chastity of her bridal bed, and had kept its vigil through the years by her hearth and in her heart. And thus love itself had not been difficult to her, for it was commanded to her and consecrated before the face of God.

And he? He wished for nothing more, knew nothing more. Indeed, what lies beyond duty would probably have seemed burdensome to him, if not actually sinful.

But there was something more! She knew it now. She had seen it in that glance, moist with yearning, lost in the light.

There was something great and ecstatic and all-powerful, something before which she quailed like a child who must go into the dark, something that she desired with every nerve and fibre.

Her eye fastened itself upon the purple square of blotting paper which looked, in the light of the lamp, like glowing metal.

She did not know how long she had sat there. It might have been minutes or hours. Often enough the morning had caught her brooding thus.

The sick man's breath came with greater diffi-- culty, his fingers grasped hers more tightly.

"Do you feel worse?" she asked.

"I am a little afraid," he said; "therefore, read me——"

He stopped, for he felt the quiver of her hand.

"You know, if you don't want to——" He was wounded in his wretched valetudinarian ego- tism, which was constantly on the scent of neg- lect.

"Oh, but I do want to; I want to do every- thing that might——"

She hurried to the table, pushed the glittering bottles aside, grasped the hymnal and read at random.

But she had to stop, for it was a prayer for rain that she had begun.

Then, as she was turning the leaves of the book, she heard the hall door of the next room open with infinite caution; she heard flying,

trembling footsteps cross the room from the balcony.

"Chut!" whispered a trembling voice.

And the door closed as with a weary moan.

What was that?

A suspicion arose in her that brought the scar-
let of shame into her cheek. The whispering next
door began anew, passionate, hasty, half-smoth-
ered by anxiety and delight. Two voices were to
be distinguished: a lighter voice which she knew,
and a duller voice, broken into, now and then, by
sonorous tones.

The letters dislimned before her eyes. The
hymn-book slipped from her hands. In utter
confusion she stared toward the door.

That really existed? Such things were possible in the world; possible among people garbed
in distinction, of careful Christian training, to
whom one looks up as to superior beings?

There was a power upon earth that could make
the delicate, radiant, distinguished woman so utterly forget shame and dignity and womanliness,
that she would open her door at midnight to a
man who had not been wedded to her in the sight
of God?

If that could happen, what was there left to
cling to in this world? Where was one's faith in
honour, fidelity, in God's grace and one's own
human worth?

A horror took hold of her so oppressive that she thought she must cry out aloud.

With a shy glance she looked at her husband. God grant that he hear nothing.

She was ashamed before him. She desired to call out, to sing, laugh, only to drown the noise of that whispering which assailed her ear like the wave of a fiery sea.

But no, he heard nothing.

His sightless eyes stared at the ceiling. He was busied with his breathing. His chest heaved and fell like a defective machine.

He didn't even expect her to read to him now. She went up to the bed and asked, listening with every nerve: "Do you want to sleep, Nathaniel?"

He lowered his eyelids in assent.

"Yes—read," he breathed.

"Shall I read softly?"

Again he assented.

"But read—don't sleep."

Fear flickered in his eyes.

"No, no," she stammered.

He motioned her to go now, and again became absorbed in the problem of breathing.

Mary took up the hymnal.

"You are to read a song of death," she said to herself, for her promise must be kept. And as though she had not understood her own admonition, she repeated: "You are to read a song of death."

But her hearing was morbidly alert, and while the golden figures on the book danced a ghostly dance before her eyes, she heard again what she desired to hear. It was like the whispering of the wind against a forbidden gate. She caught words:

"*Je t'aime — follement — j'en mourrai — je t'adore—mon amour—mon amour.*"

Mary closed her eyes. It seemed to her again as though hot waves streamed over her. And she had lost shame, too.

For there was something in all that which silenced reproach, which made this monstrous deed comprehensible, even natural. If one was so mad with love, if one felt that one could die of it!

So that existed, and was not only the lying babble of romances?

And her spirit returned and compared her own experience of love with what she witnessed now.

She had shrunk pitifully from his first kiss. When he had gone, she had embraced her mother's knees, in fear and torment at the thought of following this strange man. And she remembered how, on the evening of her wedding, her mother had whispered into her ear, "Endure, my child, and pray to God, for that is the lot of woman."

And it was that which, until to-day, she had called love.

Oh, those happy ones there, those happy ones!

"Mary," the hollow voice from the bed came.

She jumped up. " What?"

"You—don't read."

"I'll read; I'll read."

Her hands grovelled among the rough, sticky pages. An odour as of decaying foliage, which she had never noted before, came from the book. It was such an odour as comes from dark, ill-ventilated rooms, and early autumn and every-day clothes.

At last she found what she was seeking. "Ky-rie eleison! Christe eleison! Dear God, Father in heaven, have mercy upon us!"

Her lips babbled what her eyes saw, but her heart and her senses prayed another prayer: "Father in Heaven, who art love and mercy, do not count for sin to those two that which they are committing against themselves. Bless their love, even if they do not desire Thy blessing. Send faithfulness into their hearts that they cleave to one another and remain grateful for the bliss which Thou givest them. Ah, those happy ones, those happy ones!"

Tears came into her eyes. She bent her face upon the yellow leaves of the book to hide her weeping.

It seemed to her suddenly as though she understood the speech spoken in this land of eternal spring by sun and sea, by hedges of flowers and evergreen trees, by the song of birds and the laughter of man. The secret which she had sought to solve by day and by night lay suddenly revealed before her eyes.

In a sudden change of feeling her heart grew cold toward that sinful pair for which she had but just prayed. Those people became as strangers to her and sank into the mist. Their whispering died away as if it came from a great distance.

It was her own life with which she was now concerned. Gray and morose with its poverty stricken notion of duty, the past lay behind her. Bright and smiling a new world floated into her ken.

She had sworn to love him. She had cheated him. She had let him know want at her side.

Now that she knew what love was, she would reward him an hundred-fold. She, too, could love to madness, to adoration, to death. And she must love so, else she would die of famishment.

Her heart opened. Waves of tenderness, stormy, thunderous, mighty, broke forth therefrom.

Would he desire all that love? And understand it? Was he worthy of it? What did that matter?

She must give, give without measure and without reward, without thought and without will, else she would smother under all her riches.

And though he was broken and famished and mean of mind and wretched, a weakling in body and a dullard in soul; and though he lay there emaciated and gasping, a skeleton almost, moveless, half given over to dust and decay—what did it matter?

She loved him, loved him with that new and great love because he alone in all the world was her own. He was that portion of life and light and happiness which fate had given her.

She sprang up and stretched out her arms toward him.

"You my only one, my all," she whispered, folding her hands under her chin and staring at him.

His chest seemed quieter. He lay there in peace.

Weeping with happiness, she threw herself down beside him and kissed his hands. And then, as he took no notice of all that, a slow astonishment came over her. Also, she had an insecure feeling that his hand was not as usual.

Powerless to cry out, almost to breathe, she looked upon him.

She felt his forehead; she groped for his heart. All was still and cold. Then she knew.

The bell—the waiters—the physician—to what purpose? There was no need of help here. She knelt down and wanted to pray, and make up for her neglect.

A vision arose before her: the widow's house at home; her mother; the tile oven; her old maidenish sisters rattling their wooden crocheting hooks—and she herself beside them, her blonde hair smoothed with water, a little riband at her breast, gazing out upon the frozen fields, and throttling, throttling with love. For he whom fate had given her could use her love no longer.

From the next room sounded the whispering, monotonous, broken, assailing her ears in glowing waves:

"J'en mourrai—'je t'adore—mon amour."

That was his song of death. She felt that it was her own, too.

THE VICTIM

THE VICTIM

Madame Nelson, the beautiful American, had come to us from Paris, equipped with a phenomenal voice and solid Italian technique. She had immediately sung her way into the hearts of Berlin music-lovers, provided that you care to call a mixture of snobbishness, sophisticated impressionableness and goose-like imitativeness— heart. She had, therefore, been acquired by one of our most distinguished opera houses at a large salary and with long leaves of absence. I use the plural of opera house in order that no one may try to scent out the facts.

Now we had her, more especially our world of Lotharios had her. Not the younger sons of high finance, who make the boudoirs unsafe with their tall collars and short breeches; nor the bearers of ancient names who, having hung up their uniforms in the evening, assume monocle and bracelet and drag these through second and third-class drawing-rooms. No, she belonged to those worthy men of middle age, who have their palaces in the west end, whose wives one treats with infinite respect, and to whose evenings one

187

gives a final touch of elegance by singing two or three songs for nothing.

Then she committed her first folly. She went travelling with an Italian tenor. "For purposes of art," was the official version. But the time for the trip—the end of August—had been unfortunately chosen. And, as she returned ornamented with scratches administered by the tenor's pursuing wife—no one believed her.

Next winter she ruined a counsellor of a legation and magnate's son so thoroughly that he decamped to an unfrequented equatorial region, leaving behind him numerous promissory notes of questionable value.

This poor fellow was revenged the following winter by a dark-haired Roumanian fiddler, who beat her and forced her to carry her jewels to a pawnshop, where they were redeemed at half price by their original donour and used to adorn the plump, firm body of a stupid little ballet dancer.

Of course her social position was now forfeited. But then Berlin forgets so rapidly. She became proper again and returned to her earlier inclinations for gentlemen of middle life with extensive palaces and extensive wives. So there were quite a few houses—none of the strictest tone, of course—that were very glad to welcome the radiant blonde with her famous name and fragrant and modest gowns—from Paquin at ten thousand francs a piece.

At the same time she developed a remarkable business instinct. Her connections with the stock exchange permitted her to speculate without the slightest risk. For what gallant broker would let a lovely woman lose? Thus she laid the foundation of a goodly fortune, which was made to assume stately proportions by a tour through the United States, and was given a last touch of solidity by a successful speculation in Dresden real estate.

Furthermore, it would be unjust to conceal the fact that her most recent admirer, the wool manufacturer Wormser, had a considerable share in this hurtling rise of her fortunes.

Wormser guarded his good repute carefully. He insisted that his illegitimate inclinations never lack the stamp of highest elegance. He desired that they be given the greatest possible publicity at race-meets and first nights. He didn't care if people spoke with a degree of rancour, if only he was connected with the temporary lady of his heart.

Now, to be sure, there was a Mrs. Wormser. She came of a good Frankfort family. Dowry: a million and a half. She was modern to the very tips of her nervous, restless fingers.

This lady was inspired by such lofty social

ideals that she would have considered an inelegant *liaison* on her husband's part, an insult not only offered to good taste in general, but to her own in particular. Such an one she would never have forgiven. On the other hand, she approved of Madame Nelson thoroughly. She considered her the most costly and striking addition to her household. Quite figuratively, of course. Everything was arranged with the utmost propriety. At great charity festivals the two ladies exchanged a friendly glance, and they saw to it that their gowns were never made after the same model.

Then it happened that the house of Wormser was shaken. It wasn't a serious breakdown, but among the good things that had to be thrown overboard belonged—at the demand of the helping Frankforters—Madame Nelson.

And so she waited, like a virgin, for love, like a man in the weather bureau, for a given star. She felt that her star was yet to rise.

This was the situation when, one day, Herr von Karlstadt had himself presented to her. He was a captain of industry; international reputation; ennobled; the not undistinguished son of a great father. He had not hitherto been found in the market of love, but it was said of him that notable women had committed follies for his sake.

All in all, he was a man who commanded the general interest in quite a different measure from Wormser.

But artistic successes had raised Madame Nelson's name once more, too, and when news of the accomplished fact circulated, society found it hard to decide as to which of the two lent the other a more brilliant light, or which was the more to be envied.

However that was, history was richer by a famous pair of lovers.

But, just as there had been a Mrs. Wormser, so there was a Mrs. von Karlstadt.

And it is this lady of whom I wish to speak.

Mentally as well as physically Mara von Karlstadt did not belong to that class of persons which imperatively commands the attention of the public. She was sensitive to the point of madness, a little sensuous, something of an enthusiast, coquettish only in so far as good taste demanded it, and hopelessly in love with her husband. She was in love with him to the extent that she regarded the conquests which occasionally came to him, spoiled as he was, as the inevitable consequences of her fortunate choice. They inspired her with a certain woeful anger and also with a degree of pride.

The daughter of a great land owner in South Germany, she had been brought up in seclusion, and had learned only very gradually how to glide unconcernedly through the drawing-rooms. A tense smile upon her lips, which many took for irony, was only a remnant of her old diffidence. Delicate, dark in colouring, with a fine cameo-like profile, smooth hair and a tawny look in her near-sighted eyes—thus she glided about in society, and few but friends of the house took any notice of her.

And this woman who found her most genuine satisfaction in the peacefulness of life, who was satisfied if she could slip into her carriage at midnight without the annoyance of one searching glance, of one inquiring word, saw herself suddenly and without suspecting the reason, become the centre of a secret and almost insulting curiosity. She felt a whispering behind her in society; she saw from her box the lenses of many opera glasses pointing her way.

The conversation of her friends began to teem with hints, and into the tone of the men whom she knew there crept a kind of tender compassion which pained her even though she knew not how to interpret it.

For the present no change was to be noted in the demeanour of her husband. His club and his business had always kept him away from home a good deal, and if a few extra hours of absence were now added, it was easy to account for these in harmless ways, or rather, not to account for them at all, since no one made any inquiry.

Then, however, anonymous letters began to come—thick, fragrant ones with stamped coronets, and thin ones on ruled paper with the smudges of soiled fingers.

She burned the first batch; the second she handed to her husband.

The latter, who was not far from forty, and who had trained himself to an attitude of imperious brusqueness, straightened up, knotted his bushy Bismarck moustache, and said:

"Well, suppose it is true. What have you to lose?"

She did not burst into tears of despair; she did not indulge in fits of rage; she didn't even leave the room with quiet dignity; her soul seemed neither wounded nor broken. She was not even affrighted. She only thought: "I have forgiven him so much; why not forgive him this, too?"

And as she had shared him before without feeling herself degraded, so she would try to share him again.

But she soon observed that this logic of the heart would prove wanting in this instance.

In former cases she had concealed his weakness under a veil of care and considerateness. The fear of discovery had made a conscious but silent accessory of her. When it was all over she breathed deep relief at the thought: "I am the only one who even suspected."

This time all the world seemed invited to witness the spectacle.

For now she understood all that, in recent days had tortured her like an unexplained blot, an alien daub in the face which every one sees but he whom it disfigures. Now she knew what the smiling hints of her friends and the consoling desires of men had meant. Now she recognised the reason why she was wounded by the attention of all.

She was "the wife of the man whom Madame Nelson. . ."

And so torturing a shame came upon her as though she herself were the cause of the disgrace with which the world seemed to overwhelm her.

This feeling had not come upon her suddenly. At first a stabbing curiosity had awakened in her a self-torturing expectation, not without its element of morbid attraction. Daily she asked herself: "What will develope to-day?"

With quivering nerves and cramped heart, she entered evening after evening, for the season was at its height, the halls of strangers on her husband's arm.

And it was always the same thing. The same glances that passed from her to him and from him to her, the same compassionate sarcasm upon averted faces, the same hypocritical delicacy in conversation, the same sudden silence as soon as she turned to any group of people to listen—the same cruel pillory for her evening after evening, night after night.

And if all this had not been, she would have felt it just the same.

And in these drawing-rooms there were so many women whose husbands' affairs were the talk of the town. Even her predecessor, Mrs. Wormser, had passed over the expensive immorality of her husband with a self-sufficing smile and a condescending jest, and the world had bowed down to her respectfully, as it always does when scenting a temperament that it is powerless to wound.

Why had this martyrdom come to her, of all people?

Thus, half against her own will, she began to hide, to refuse this or that invitation, and to spend the free evenings in the nursery, watching over the sleep of her boys and weaving dreams of a new happiness. The illness of her older child gave her an excuse for withdrawing from society altogether and her husband did not restrain her.

It had never come to an explanation between them, and as he was always considerate, even tender, and as sharp speeches were not native to her temper, the peace of the home was not disturbed.

Soon it seemed to her, too, as though the rude inquisitiveness of the world were slowly passing away. Either one had abandoned the critical condition of her wedded happiness for more vivid topics, or else she had become accustomed to the state of affairs.

She took up a more social life, and the shame which she had felt in appearing publicly with her husband gradually died out.

What did not die out, however, was a keen desire to know the nature and appearance of the woman in whose hands lay her own destiny. How did she administer the dear possession that fate had put in her power? And when and how would she give it back?

She threw aside the last remnant of reserve and questioned friends. Then, when she was met by a smile of compassionate ignorance, she asked women. These were more ready to report. But she would not and could not believe what she was told. He had surely not degraded himself into being one of a succession of moneyed rakes. It was clear to her that, in order to soothe her grief, people slandered the woman and him with her.

In order to watch her secretly, she veiled heavily and drove to the theatre where Madame Nelson was singing. Shadowlike she cowered in the depths of a box which she had rented under an assumed name and followed with a kind of pained voluptuousness the ecstasies of love which the other woman, fully conscious of the victorious loveliness of her body, unfolded for the benefit of the breathless crowd.

With such an abandoned raising of her radiant arms, she threw herself upon *his* breast; with that curve of her modelled limbs, she lay before *his* knees.

And in her awakened a reverent, renouncing envy of a being who had so much to give, beside whom she was but a dim and poor shadow, weary with motherhood, corroded with grief.

At the same time there appeared a California mine owner, a multi-millionaire, with whom her husband had manifold business dealings. He introduced his daughters into society and himself gave a number of luxurious dinners at which he tried to assemble guests of the most exclusive character.

Just as they were about to enter a carriage to drive to the "Bristol," to one of these dinners, a message came which forced Herr von Karlstadt to take an immediate trip to his factories. He begged his wife to go instead, and she did not refuse.

The company was almost complete and the

daughter of the mine owner was doing the honours of the occasion with appropriate grace when the doors of the reception room opened for the last time and through the open doorway floated rather than walked—Madame Nelson.

The petrified little group turned its glance of inquisitive horror upon Mrs. von Karlstadt, while the mine owner's daughter adjusted the necessary introductions with a grand air.

Should she go or not? No one was to be found who would offer her his arm. Her feet were paralysed. And she remained.

The company sat down at table. And since fate, in such cases, never does its work by halves, it came to pass that Madame Nelson was assigned to a seat immediately opposite her.

The people present seemed grateful to her that they had not been forced to witness a scene, and overwhelmed her with delicate signs of this gratitude. Slowly her self-control returned to her. She dared to look about her observantly, and, behold, Madame Nelson appealed to her.

Her French was faultless, her manners equally so, and when the Californian drew her into the conversation, she practised the delicate art of modest considerateness to the extent of talking past Mrs. von Karlstadt in such a way that those who did not know were not enlightened and those who knew felt their anxiety depart.

In order to thank her for this alleviation of a fatally painful situation, Mrs. von Karlstadt occasionally turned perceptibly toward the singer. For this Madame Nelson was grateful in her turn. Thus their glances began to meet in friendly fashion, their voices to cross, the atmosphere became less constrained from minute to minute, and when the meal was over the astonished assembly had come to the conclusion that Mrs. von Karlstadt was ignorant of the true state of affairs.

The news of this peculiar meeting spread like a conflagration. Her women friends hastened to congratulate her on her strength of mind; her male friends praised her loftiness of spirit. She went through the degradation which she had suffered as though it were a triumph. Only her husband went about for a time with an evil conscience and a frowning forehead.

Months went by. The quietness of summer intervened, but the memory of that evening rankled in her and blinded her soul. Slowly the thought arose in her which was really grounded in vanity, but looked, in its execution, like suffering love—the thought that she would legitimise her husband's irregularity in the face of society.

Hence when the season began again she wrote a letter to Madame Nelson in which she invited her, in a most cordial way, to sing at an approaching function in her home. She proffered this request, not only in admiration of the singer's gifts, but also, as she put it, "to render nugatory a persistent and disagreeable rumour."

Madame Nelson, to whom this chance of repairing her fair fame was very welcome, had the indiscretion to assent, and even to accept the condition of entire secrecy in regard to the affair.

The chronicler may pass over the painful evening in question with suitable delicacy of touch. Nothing obvious or crass took place. Madame Nelson sang three enchanting songs, accompanied by a first-rate pianist. A friend of the house of whom the hostess had requested this favour took Madame Nelson to the *buffet*. A number of guileless individuals surrounded that lady with hopeful adoration. An ecstatic mood prevailed. The one regrettable feature of the occasion was that the host had to withdraw—as quietly as possible, of course—on account of a splitting headache.

Berlin society, which felt wounded in the innermost depth of its ethics, never forgave the Karlstadts for this evening. I believe that in certain circles the event is still remembered, although years have passed.

Its immediate result, however, was a breach between man and wife.

Mara went to the Riviera, where she remained until spring.

An apparent reconciliation was then patched up, but its validity was purely external.

Socially, too, things readjusted themselves, although people continued to speak of the Karlstadt house with a smile that asked for indulgence.

Mara felt this acutely, and while her husband appeared oftener and more openly with his mistress, she withdrew into the silence of her inner chambers.

Then she took a lover.

Or, rather, she was taken by him.

A lonely evening . . . A fire in the chimney . . . A friend who came in by accident . . The same friend who had taken care of Madame Nelson for her on that memorable evening . . . The fall of snow without . . . A burst of confidence . . . A sob . . . A nestling against the caressing hand . . . It was done . . .

Months passed. She experienced not one hour of intoxication, not one of that inner absolution which love brings. It was moral slackness and weariness that made her yield again. . .

Then the consequences appeared.

Of course, the child could not, must not, be born. And it was not born.

One can imagine the horror of that tragic time: the criminal flame of sleepless nights, the blood-charged atmosphere of guilty despair, the moans of agony that had to be throttled behind closed doors.

What remained to her was lasting invalidism. The way from her bed to an invalid's chair was long and hard.

Time passed. Improvements came and gave place to lapses in her condition. Trips to watering-places alternated with visits to sanatoriums.

In those places sat the pallid, anæmic women who had been tortured and ruined by their own or alien guilt. There they sat and engaged in wretched flirtations with flighty neurasthenics.

And gradually things went from bad to worse. The physicians shrugged their friendly shoulders.

And then it happened that Madame Nelson felt the inner necessity of running away with a handsome young tutor. She did this less out of passion than to convince the world—after having thoroughly fleeced it—of the unselfishness of her feelings. For it was her ambition to be counted among the great lovers of all time.

One evening von Karlstadt entered the sick chamber of his wife, sat down beside her bed and silently took her hand.

She was aware of everything, and asked with a gentle smile upon her white lips:

"Be frank with me: did you love her, at least?"

He laughed shrilly. "What should have made me love this—business lady?"

They looked at each other long. Upon her face death had set its seal. His hair was gray, his self-respect broken, his human worth squandered. . .

And then, suddenly, they clung to each other, and leaned their foreheads against each other, and wept.

AUTUMN

AUTUMN

AUTUMN

I.

Iᴛ was on a sunny afternoon in October.
Human masses streamed through the alleys of
the *Tiergarten*. With the desperate passion of
an ageing woman who feels herself about to be
deserted, the giant city received the last caresses
of summer. A dotted throng that was not unlike the chaos of the *Champs Élysées,* filled the
broad, gray road that leads to Charlottenburg.

Berlin, which cannot compete with any other
great European city, as far as the luxury of
vehicular traffic is concerned, seemed to have sent
out to-day all it possessed in that kind. The
weather was too beautiful for closed *coupés,* and
hence the comfortable family landau was most in
evidence. Only now and then did an elegant
victoria glide along, or an aristocratic four-in-
hand demand the respectful yielding of the
crowd.

A dog-cart of dark yellow, drawn by a magnificent trotter, attracted the attention of ex-
perts. The noble animal, which seemed to feel

the security of the guiding hand, leaned, snorting, upon its bit. With far out-reaching hind legs, it flew along, holding its neck moveless, as became a scion of its race.

The man who drove was sinewy, tall, about forty, with clear, gray eyes, sharply cut profile and a close-clipped moustache. In his thin, brownish cheeks were several deep scars, and between the straight, narrow brows could be seen two salient furrows.

His attire—an asphalt-gray, thick-seamed overcoat, a coloured shirt and red gloves—did not deny the sportsman. His legs, which pressed against the footboard, were clad in tight, yellow riding boots.

Many people saluted him. He returned their salutations with that careless courtesy which belongs to those who know themselves to have transcended the judgment of men.

If one of his acquaintances happened to be accompanied by a lady, he bowed deeply and respectfully, but without giving the ladies in question a single glance.

People looked after him and mentioned his name: Baron von Stueckrath.

Ah, that fellow. . .

And they looked around once more.

At the square of the *Great Star* he turned to the left, drove along the river, passed the well-known resort called simply *The Tents,* and stopped not far from the building of the general staff of the army and drew up before a large distinguished house with a fenced front garden and cast-iron gate to the driveway.

He threw the reins to the groom, who sat statuesquely behind him, and said: "Drive home."

Jumping from the cart, he observed the handle of the scraper sticking in the top of one of his boots. He drew it out, threw it on the seat, and entered the house.

The janitor, an old acquaintance, greeted him with the servile intimacy of the tip-expecting tribe.

On the second floor he stopped and pulled the bell whose glass knob glittered above a neat brass plate.

"Ludovika Kraissl," was engraved upon it.

A maid, clad with prim propriety in a white apron and white lace cap, opened the door.

He entered and handed her his hat.

"Is Madame at home?"

"No, sir."

He looked at her through half-closed lids, and observed how her milk-white little madonna's face flushed to the roots of her blonde hair.

"Where did she go?"

"Madame meant to go to the dressmaker," the girl stuttered, "and to make some purchases."

She avoided his eyes. She had been in service only three months and had not yet perfected herself in lying.

He whistled a tune between his set teeth and entered the drawing-room.

A penetrating perfume streamed forth.

"Open the window, Meta."

She passed noiselessly through the room and executed his command.

Frowning, he looked about him. The empty pomp of the light woman offended his taste. The creature who lived here had a gift for filling every corner with banal and tasteless trivialities.

When he had turned over the flat to her it had been a charming little place, full of delicate tints and the simple lines of Louis Seize furniture. In a few years she had made a junk shop of it.

"Would you care for tea, sir, or anything else?" the girl asked.

"No, thank you. Pull off my boots, Meta. I'll change my dress and then go out again."

Modestly, almost humbly, she bowed before him and set his spurred foot gently on her lap. Then she loosened the top straps. He let his glance rest, well pleased, upon her smooth, silvery blonde hair.

How would it work if he sent his mistress packing and installed this girl in her place?

But he immediately abandoned the thought.

He had seen the thing done by some of his friends. In a single year the chastest and most modest servant girl was so thoroughly corrupted that she had to be driven into the streets.

"We men seem to emit a pestilential air," he reflected, "that corrupts every woman."

"Or at least men of my kind," he added carefully.

"Have you any other wishes, sir?" asked the girl, daintily wiping her hands on her apron.

"No, thank you."

She turned to the door.

"One thing more, Meta. When did Madame say she would be back?"

Her face was again mantled with blood.

"She didn't say anything definite. I was to make her excuses. She intended to return home by evening, at all events."

He nodded and the girl went with a sigh of relief, gently closing the door behind her.

He continued to whistle, and looked up at a hanging lamp, which defined itself against the window niche by means of a wreath of gay artificial flowers.

In this hanging lamp, which hung there unnoticed and unreachable from the floor, he had, a year ago, quite by accident, discovered a store of love letters. His mistress had concealed them there since she evidently did not even consider the secret drawer of her desk a sufficiently safe repository.

He had carefully kept the secret of the lamp to himself, and had only fed his grim humour from time to time by observing the changes of her heart by means of added missives. In this way he had been able to observe the number of his excellent friends with whom she deceived him.

Thus his contempt for mankind assumed monstrous proportions, but this contempt was the one emotional luxury which his egoism was still capable of.

He grasped a chair and seemed, for a moment about to mount to the lamp to inspect her latest history. But he let his hand fall. After all, it was indifferent with whom she was unfaithful to-day. . .

And he was tired. A bad day's work lay behind him. A three-year-old full-blooded horse, recently imported from Hull, had proven itself abnormally sensitive and had brought him to the verge of despair by its fearfulness and its moods. He had exercised it for hours, and had only succeeded in making the animal more nervous than before. Great sums were at stake if the fault should prove constitutional and not curable.

He felt the impulse to share his worries with some one, but he knew of no one. From the point of view of Miss Ludi's naïve selfishness, it was simply his duty to be successful. She didn't care for the troublesome details. At his club, again, each one was warily guarding his own interests. Hence it was necessary there to speak carefully, since an inadvertent expression might affect general opinion.

He almost felt impelled to call in the maid and speak to her of his worries.

Then his own softness annoyed him.

It was his wont to pass through life in lordly isolation and to astonish the world by his successes. That was all he needed.

Yawning he stretched himself out on the *chaise longue*. Time dragged.

Three hours would pass until Ludi's probable return. He was so accustomed to the woman's society that he almost longed for her. Her idle chatter helped him. Her little tricks refreshed him. But the most important point was this: she was no trouble. He could caress her or beat her, call to her and drive her from him like a little dog. He could let her feel the full measure of his contempt, and she would not move a muscle. She was used to nothing else.

He passed two or three hours daily in her company, for time had to be killed somehow. Sometimes, too, he took her to the circus or the theatre. He had long broken with the families of his acquaintance and could appear in public with light women.

And yet he felt a sharp revulsion at the atmosphere that surrounded him. A strange discomfort invaded his soul in her presence. He didn't feel degraded. He knew her to be a harlot. But that was what he wanted. None but such an one would permit herself to be so treated. It was rather a disguised discouragement that held him captive.

Was life to pass thus unto the very end? Was life worth living, if it offered a favourite of fortune, a master of his will and of his actions, nothing better than this?

"Surely I have the spleen," he said to himself, sprang up, and went into the next room to change his clothes. He had a wardrobe in Ludi's dressing room in order to be able to go out from here in the evening unrestrainedly.

II.

It was near four o'clock.

The sun laughed through the window. Its light was deep purple, changing gradually to violet. Masses of leaves, red as rust, gleamed over from the *Tiergarten.* The figure of Victory upon the triumphal column towered toward heaven like a mighty flame.

He felt an impulse to wander through the alleys of the park idly and aimlessly, at most to give a coin to a begging child.

He left the house and went past the Moltke monument and the winding ways that lead to the Charlottenburg road.

The ground exhaled the sweetish odour of decaying plants. Rustling heaps of leaves, which the breezes of noon had swept together, flew apart under his tread. The westering sun threw red splotches of light on the faint green of the tree trunks that exuded their moisture in long streaks.

Here it was lonely. Only beyond the great road, whose many-coloured pageant passed by him like a kinematograph, did he hear again in the alleys the sounds of children's voices, song and laughter.

In the neighbourhood of the *Rousseau Island* he met a gentleman whom he knew and who had been a friend of his youth. Stout of form, his round face surrounded by a close-clipped beard, he wandered along, leading two little girls in red, while a boy in a blue sailor suit rode ahead, herald-like, on his father's walking-stick.

The two men bowed to each other coolly, but without ill-will. They were simply estranged. The busy servant of the state and father of a family was scarcely to be found in those circles were the daily work consists in riding and betting and gambling.

Stueckrath sat down on a bench and gazed after the group. The little red frocks gleamed through the bushes, and Papa's admonishing and restraining voice was to be heard above the noise of the boy who made a trumpet of his hollow hand.

"Is that the way happiness looks?" he asked himself. "Can a man of energy and action find satisfaction in these banal domesticities?"

And strangely enough, these fathers of families, men who serve the state and society, who occupy high offices, make important inventions and write good books—these men have red cheeks and laughing eyes. They do not look as though the burden which they carry squeezes the breath of life out of them. They get ahead, in spite of the childish hands that cling to their coats, in spite of the trivialities with which they pass their hours of leisure.

An indeterminate feeling of envy bored into his soul. He fought it down and went on, right into the throng that filled the footpaths of the *Tiergarten*. Groups of ladies from the west end went by him in rustling gowns of black. He did not know them and did not wish to know them.

Here, too, he recognized fewer of the men. The financiers who have made this quarter their own appear but rarely at the races.

Accompanying carriages kept pace with the promenaders in order to explain and excuse their unusual exertion. For in this world the continued absence of one's carriage may well shake one's credit.

The trumpeting motor-cars whirred by with gleaming brasses. Of the beautiful women in them, little could be seen in the swift gleams. It was the haste of a new age that does not even find time to display its vanity.

Upon the windows of the villas and palaces opposite lay the iridescent glow of the evening sun. The façades took on purple colours, and the decaying masses of vines that weighed heavily upon the fences seemed to glow and shine from within with the very phosphorescence of decay.

Flooded by this light, a slender, abnormally tall girl came into Stueckrath's field of vision. She led by the arm an aged lady, who hobbled with difficulty along the pebbly path. A closed carriage with escutcheon and coronet followed the two slowly.

He stopped short. An involuntary movement had passed through his body, an impulse to turn off into one of the side paths. But he conquered himself at once, and looked straight at the approaching ladies.

Like a mere line of blackness, thin of limb and waist, attired with nun-like austerity in garments that hung as if withering upon her, she stood against the background of autumnal splendour.

Now she recognised him, too. A sudden redness that at once gave way to lifeless pallor flashed across her delicate, stern face.

They looked straight into each other's eyes.

He bowed deeply. She smiled with an effort at indifference.

"And so she is faded, too," he thought. To be sure, her face still bore the stamp of a simple and severe beauty, but time and grief had dealt ungently with it. The lips were pale and anæmic, two or three folds, sharp as if made with a knife, surrounded them. About the eyes, whose soft

and lambent light of other days had turned into
a hard and troubled sharpness, spread concentric
rings, united by a network of veins and wrinkles.

He stood still, lost in thought, and looked
after her.

She still trod the earth like a queen, but her
outline was detestable.

Only hopelessness bears and attires itself thus.

He calculated. She must be thirty-six. Thir-
teen years ago he had known her and—loved her?
Perhaps. . .

At least he had left her the evening before
their formal betrothal was to take place because
her father had dared to remark upon his way of
life.

He loved his personal liberty more than his
beautiful and wealthy betrothed who clung to
him with every fibre of her delicate and noble
soul. One word from her, had it been but a
word of farewell, would have recalled him. That
word remained unspoken.

Thus her life's happiness had been wrecked.
Perhaps his, too. What did it matter?

Since then he had nothing but contempt for
the daughters of good families. Other women
were less exacting; they did not attempt to cir-
cumscribe his freedom.

He gazed after her long. Now groups of
other pedestrians intervened; now her form re-

appeared sharp and narrow against the trees. From time to time she stooped lovingly toward the old lady, who, as is the wont of aged people, trod eagerly and fearfully.

This fragile heap of bones, with the dull eyes and the sharp voice—he remembered the voice well: it had had part in his decision. This strange, unsympathetic, suspicious old woman, he would have had to call "Mother."

What madness! What hypocrisy!

And yet his hunger for happiness, which had not yet died, reminded him of all that might have been.

A sea of warm, tender and unselfish love would have flooded him and fructified and vivified the desert of his soul. And instead of becoming withered and embittered, she would have blossomed at his side more richly from day to day.

Now it was too late. A long, thin, wretched little creature—she went her way and was soon lost in the distance.

But there clung to his soul the yearning for a woman—one who had more of womanliness than its name and its body, more than the harlot whom he kept because he was too slothful to drive her from him.

He sought the depths of his memory. His life had been rich in gallant adventures. Many a full-blooded young woman had thrown herself at him, and had again vanished from his life under the compulsion of his growing coldness.

He loved his liberty. Even an unlawful relation felt like a fetter so soon as it demanded any sacrifice of time or interests. Also, he did not like to give less than he received. For, since the passing of his unscrupulous youth, he had not cared to receive the gift of a human destiny only to throw it aside as his whim demanded.

And therefore his life had grown quiet during the last few years.

He thought of one of his last loves . . . the very last . . . and smiled.

The image of a delicately plump brunette little woman, with dreamy eyes and delicious little curls around her ears, rose up before him. She dwelt in his memory as she had seemed to him: modest, soulful, all ecstatic yielding and charming simple-heartedness.

She did not belong to society. He had met her at a dinner given by a financial magnate. She was the wife of an upper clerk who was well respected in the business world. With adoring curiosity, she peeped into the great strange world, whose doors opened to her for the first time.

He took her to the table, was vastly entertained by the lack of sophistication with which she received all these new impressions, and smilingly accepted the undisguised adoration with which she regarded him in his character of a famous horseman and rake.

He flirted with her a bit and that turned her head completely. In lonely dreams her yearning for elegant and phantastic sin had grown to enormity. She was now so wholly and irresistibly intoxicated that he received next morning a deliciously scribbled note in which she begged him for a secret meeting—somewhere in the neighbourhood of the *Arkona Place* or *Weinmeisterstrasse,* regions as unknown to him as the North Cape or Yokohama.

Two or three meetings followed. She appeared, modest, anxious and in love, a bunch of violets for his button-hole in her hand, and some surprise for her husband in her pocket.

Then the affair began to bore him and he refused an appointment.

One evening, during the last days of November, she appeared, thickly veiled, in his dwelling, and sank sobbing upon his breast. She could not live without seeing him; she was half crazed with longing; he was to do with her what he would. He consoled her, warmed her, and kissed the melting snow from her hair. But when in his joy at what he considered the full possession of a jewel his tenderness went beyond hers, her conscience smote her. She was an honest woman. Horror and shame would drive her into her grave if she went hence an adulteress. He must have pity on her and be content with her pure adoration.

He had the requisite pity, dismissed her with a paternal kiss upon her forehead, but at the same time ordered his servant to admit her no more.

Then came two or three letters. In her agony over the thought of losing him, she was willing to break down the last reserve. But he did not answer the letters.

At the same time the thought came to him of going up the Nile in a dahabiyeh. He was bored and had a cold.

On the evening of his departure he found her waiting in his rooms.

"What do you want?"

"Take me along."

"How do you know?"

"Take me along."

She said nothing else.

The necessity of comforting her was clear. A thoroughgoing farewell was celebrated, with the understanding that it was a farewell forever.

The pact had been kept. After his return and for two years more she had given no sign of life.

He now thought of this woman. He felt a poignant longing for the ripe sweetness of her oval face, the veiled depth of her voice. He desired once more to be embraced by her firm arms, to be kissed by her mad, hesitating lips.

Why had he dropped her? How could he have abandoned her so rudely?

The thought came into his head of looking her up now, in this very hour.

He had a dim recollection of the whereabouts of her dwelling. He could soon ascertain its exact situation.

Then again the problems of his racing stable came into his head. The thought of "Maidenhood," the newly purchased horse, worried him. He had staked much upon one throw. If he lost, it would take time to repair the damage.

Suddenly he found himself in a tobacconist's shop, looking for her name in the directory. *Friedrich-Wilhelm Strasse* was the address. Quite near, as he had surmised.

He was not at loss for an excuse. Her husband must still be in his office at this hour. He would not be asked for any very strict accounting for his action. At worst there was an approaching riding festival, for which he could request her coöperation.

Perhaps she had forgotten him and would revenge herself for her humiliation. Perhaps she would be insulted and not even receive him. At best he must count upon coldness, bitter truths and that appearance of hatred which injured love assumes.

What did it matter? She was a woman, after all.

The vestibule of the house was supported by pillars; its walls were ornately stuccoed; the floor was covered with imitation oriental rugs. It was the rented luxury with which the better middle-class loves to surround itself.

He ascended three flights of stairs.

An elderly servant in a blue apron regarded the stranger suspiciously.

He asked for her mistress.

She would see. Holding his card gingerly, she disappeared.

Now *he* would see. . .

Then, as he bent forward, listening, he heard through the open door a cry—not of horrified surprise, but of triumph and jubilation, such a cry of sudden joy as only a long and hopeless and unrestrainable yearning can send forth.

He thought he had heard wrong, but the smiling face of the returning servant reassured him.

He was to be made welcome.

III.

HE entered. With outstretched hands, tears in her eyes, her face a-quiver with a vain attempt at equanimity—thus she came forward to meet him.

"There you are . . . there you are . . . you. . ."

Overwhelmed and put to shame by her forgiveness and her happiness, he stood before her in silence.

What could he have said to her that would not have sounded either coarse or trivial?

And she demanded neither explanation nor excuse.

He was here—that was enough for her.

As he let his glance rest upon her, he confessed that his mental image of her fell short of the present reality.

She had grown in soul and stature. Her features bore signs of power and restraint, and of a strong inner tension. Her eyes sought him with a steady light; in her bosom battled the pent-up joy.

She asked him to be seated.

"In that corner," she said, and led him to a tiny sofa covered with glittering, light-green silk, above which hung a withered palm-leaf fan.

"I have sat there so often," she went on, "so often, and have thought of you, always—always. You'll drink tea, won't you?"

He was about to refuse, but she interrupted him.

"Oh, but you must, you must. You can't refuse! It has been my dream all this time to drink tea with you here just once—just once. To serve you on this little table and hand you the basket with cakes! Do you see this little lacquer table, with the lovely birds of inlaid mother-of-pearl? I had that given to me last Christmas for the especial purpose of serving you tea on it. For I said to myself: 'He is accustomed to the highest elegance.' And you are here and are going to refuse? No, no, that's impossible. I couldn't bear that."

And she flew to the door and called out her orders to the servant.

He regarded her in happy astonishment. In all her movements there was a rhythm of unconscious loveliness, such as he had rarely seen in any woman. With simple, unconscious elegance, her dress flowed about her taller figure, whose severe lines were softened by the womanly curves of her limbs.

And all that belonged to him.

He could command this radiant young body and this radiant young soul. All that was one hunger to be possessed by him.

"Bind her to yourself," cried his soul, "and build yourself a new happiness!"

Then she returned. She stopped a few paces from him, folded her hands under her chin, gazed at him wide-eyed and whispered: "There he is! There he is!"

He grew uncomfortable under this expense of passion.

"I should wager that I sit here with a foolish face," he thought.

"But now I'm going to be sensible," she went on, sitting down on a low stool that stood next to the sofa. "And while the tea is steeping you must tell me how things have gone with you all this long time. For it is a very long time since . . . Ah, a long time. . ."

It seemed to him that there was a reproach behind these words. He gave but a dry answer to her question, but threw the more warmth into his inquiries concerning her life.

She laughed and waved her hand.

"Oh, I!" she cried. "I have fared admirably. Why should I not? Life makes me as happy as though I were a child. Oh, I can always be happy. . . That's characteristic of me. Nearly

every day brings something new and usually
something delightful. . . And since I've been in
love with you. . . You mustn't take that for a
banal declaration of passion, dear friend. . .
Just imagine you are merely my confidant, and
that I'm telling you of my distant lover who
takes little notice of a foolish woman like myself.
But then, that doesn't matter so long as I
know that he is alive and can fear and pray for
him; so long as the same morning sun shines on
us both. Why, do you know, it's a most delicious
feeling, when the morning is fair and the sun
golden and one may stand at the window and
say: 'Thank God, it is a beautiful day for
him.' "

He passed his hand over his forehead.

"It isn't possible," he thought. "Such things
don't exist in this world."

And she went on, not thinking that perhaps
he, too, would want to speak.

"I don't know whether many people have the
good fortune to be as happy as I. But I am,
thank God. And do you know, the best part of
it all and the sunniest, I owe to you. For instance: Summer before last we went to Heligoland, last summer to Schwarzburg. . . Do you
know it? Isn't it beautiful? Well, for instance:
I wake up; I open my eyes to the dawn. I get
up softly, so as not to disturb my husband, and

go on my bare feet to the window. Without, the wooded mountains lie dark and peaceful. There is a peace over it all that draws one's tears . . . it is so beautiful . . . and behind, on the horizon, there shines a broad path of gold. And the fir-trees upon the highest peaks are sharply defined against the gold, like little men with many out-stretched arms. And already the early piping of a few birds is heard. And I fold my hands and think: I wonder where he is . . . And if he is asleep, has he fair dreams? Ah, if he were here and could see all this loveliness. And I think of *him* with such impassioned intensity that it is not hard to believe him here and able to see it all. And at last a chill comes up, for it is always cool in the mountains, as you know. . . And then one slips back into bed, and is annoyed to think that one must sleep four hours more instead of being up and thinking of him. And when one wakes up for a second time, the sun throws its golden light into the windows, and the breakfast table is set on the balcony. And one's husband has been up quite a while, but waits patiently. And his dear, peaceful face is seen through the glass door. At such moments one's heart ex-pands in gratitude to God who has made life so beautiful and one can hardly bear one's own hap piness—and—there is the tea."

The elderly maid came in with a salver, which

she placed on the piano, in order to set the little table properly. A beautiful napkin of damask silk lay ready. The lady of the house scolded jestingly. It would injure the polish of the piano, and what was her guest to think of such shiftlessness.

The maid went out.

She took up the tea-kettle, and asked in a voice full of bliss.

"Strong or weak, dear master?"

"Strong, please."

"One or two lumps of sugar?"

"Two lumps, please."

She passed him the cup with a certain solemnity.

"So this is the great moment, the pinnacle of all happiness as I have dreamed of it! Now, tell me yourself: Am I not to be envied? Whatever I wish is fulfilled. And, do you know, last year in Heligoland I had a curious experience. We capsised by the dunes and I fell into the water. As I lost consciousness, I thought that you were there and were saving me. Later when I lay on the beach, I saw, of course, that it had been only a stupid old fisherman. But the feeling was so wonderful while it lasted that I almost felt like jumping into the water again. Speaking of water, do you take rum in your tea?"

He shook his head. Her chatter, which at

first had enraptured him, began to fill him with sadness. He did not know how to respond. His youthfulness and flexibility of mind had passed from him long ago: he had long lost any inner cheerfulness.

And while she continued to chat, his thoughts wandered, like a horse, on their accustomed path on the road of his daily worries. He thought of an unsatisfactory jockey, of the nervous horse.

What was this woman to him, after all?

"By the way," he heard her say, "I wanted to ask you whether 'Maidenhood' has arrived?"

He sat up sharply and stared at her. Surely he had heard wrong.

"What do you know about 'Maidenhood'?"

"But, my dear friend, do you suppose I haven't heard of your beautiful horse, by 'Blue Devil' out of 'Nina'? Now, do you see? I believe I know the grandparents, too. Anyhow, you are to be congratulated on your purchase. The English trackmen are bursting with envy. To judge by that, you ought to have an immense success."

"But, for heaven's sake, how do you know all this?"

"Dear me, didn't your purchase appear in all the sporting papers?"

"Do you read those papers?"

"Surely. You see, here is the last number of

the *Spur,* and yonder is the bound copy of the
German Sporting News."

"I see; but to what purpose?"

"Oh, I'm a sporting lady, dear master. I look
upon the world of horses—is that the right expression?—with benevolent interest. I hope that
isn't forbidden?"

"But you never told me a word about that before!"

She blushed a little and cast her eyes down.

"Oh, before, before. . . That interest didn't
come until later."

He understood and dared not understand.

"Don't look at me so," she besought him;
there's nothing very remarkable about it. I just
said to myself: Well, if he doesn't want you, at
least you can share his life from afar. That isn't
immodest, is it? And then the race meets were
the only occasions on which I could see you from
afar. And whenever you yourself rode—oh, how
my heart beat—fit to burst. And when you won,
oh, how proud I was! I could have cried out my
secret for all the world to hear. And my poor
husband's arm was always black and blue. I
pinched him first in my anxiety and then in my
joy."

"So your husband happily shares your enthusiasm?"

"Oh, at first he wasn't very willing. But then,

he is so good, so good. And as I couldn't go to the races alone, why he just had to go with me! And in the end he has become as great an enthusiast as I am. We can sit together for hours and discuss the tips. And he just admires you so— almost more than I. Oh, how happy he'd be to meet you here. You mustn't refuse him that pleasure. And now you're laughing at me. Shame on you!"

"I give you my word that nothing——"

"Oh, but you smiled. I saw you smile."

"Perhaps. But assuredly with no evil intention. And now you'll permit me to ask a serious question, won't you?"

"But surely!"

"Do you love your husband?"

"Why, of course I love him. You don't know him, or you wouldn't ask. How could I help it? We're like two children together. And I don't mean anything silly. We're like that in hours of grief, too. Sometimes when I look at him in his sleep—the kind, careworn forehead, the silent serious mouth—and when I think how faithfully and carefully he guides me, how his one dreaming and waking thought is for my happiness— why, then I kneel down and kiss his hands till he wakes up. Once he thought it was our little dog, and murmured 'Shoo, shoo!' Oh, how we laughed! And if you imagine that such a state of affairs can't be reconciled with my feeling for you, why, then you're quite wrong. *That* is upon an entirely different plane."

"And your life is happy?"

"Perfectly, perfectly."

Radiantly she folded her hands.

She did not suspect her position on the fearful edge of an abyss. She had not yet realised what his coming meant, nor how defenceless she was.

He had but to stretch out his arms and she would fly to him, ready to sacrifice her fate to his mood. And this time there would be no returning to that well-ordered content.

A dull feeling of responsibility arose in him and paralysed his will. Here was all that he needed in order to conquer a few years of new freshness and joy for the arid desert of his life. Here was the spring of life for which he was athirst. And he had not the courage to touch it with his lips.

IV.

A SILENCE ensued in which their mood threatened to darken and grow turbid.

Then he pulled himself together.

"You don't ask me why I came, dear friend."

She shrugged her shoulders and smiled.

"A moment's impulse—or loneliness. That's all."

"And a bit of remorse, don't you think so?"

"Remorse? For what? You have nothing with which to reproach yourself. Was not our agreement made to be kept?"

"And yet I couldn't wholly avoid the feeling as if my unbroken silence must have left a sting in your soul which would embitter your memory of me."

Thoughtfully she stirred her tea.

"No," she said at last, "I'm not so foolish. The memory of you is a sacred one. If that were not so, how could I have gone on living? That time, to be sure, I wanted to take my life. I had determined on that before I came to you. For that one can leave the man with whom. . . I never thought that possible. . . But one learns

a good deal—a good deal. . . And now I'll tell
you how it came to pass that I didn't take my life
that night. When everything was over, and I
stood in the street before your house, I said to
myself: 'Now the river is all that is left.' In
spite of rain and storm, I took an open cab and
drove out to the *Tiergarten*. Wasn't the weather
horrible! At the *Great Star* I left the cab and
ran about in the muddy ways, weeping, weeping.
I was blind with tears, and lost my way. I said
to myself that I would die at six. There were
still four minutes left. I asked a policeman the
way to *Bellevue,* for I did remember that the
river flows hard behind the castle. The policeman said: 'There it is. The hour is striking in
the tower now.' And when I heard the clock
strike, the thought came to me: 'Now my husband is coming home, tired and hungry, and I'm
not there. If at least he wouldn't let his dinner
get cold. But of course he will wait. He'd
rather starve than eat without me. And he'll be
frightened more and more as the hours pass.
Then he'll run to the police. And next morning
he'll be summoned by telegram to the morgue.
There he'll break down helplessly and hopelessly
and I won't be able to console him.' And when
I saw that scene in my mind, I called out: 'Cab!
cab!' But there was no cab. So I ran back to
the *Great Star,* and jumped into the street-car,

and rode home and rushed into his arms and cried my fill."

"And had your husband no questions to ask? Did he entertain no suspicion?"

"Oh, no, he knows me. I am taken that way sometimes. If anything moves or delights me deeply—a lovely child on the street—you see, I haven't any—or some glorious music, or sometimes only the park in spring and some white statue in the midst of the greenery. Oh, sometimes I seem to feel my very soul melt, and then he lays his cool, firm hand on my forehead and I am healed."

"And were you healed on that occasion, too?"

"Yes. I was calmed at once. 'Here,' I said to myself, 'is this dear, good man, to whom you can be kind. And as far as the other is concerned, why it was mere mad egoism to hope to have a share in his life. For to give love means, after all, to demand love. And what can a poor, supersensitive thing like you mean to him? He has others. He need but stretch forth his hand, and the hearts of countesses and princesses are his!' "

"Dear God," he thought, and saw the image of the purchasable harlot, who was supposed to satisfy his heart's needs.

But she chatted on, and bit by bit built up for him the image of him which she had cherished during these two years. All the heroes of Byron, Poushkine, Spielhagen and Scott melted into one glittering figure. There was no splendour of earth with which her generous imagination had not dowered him.

He listened with a melancholy smile, and thought: "Thank God, she doesn't know me. If I didn't take a bit of pleasure in my stable, the contrast would be too terrible to contemplate."

And there was nothing forward, nothing immodest, in this joyous enthusiasm. It was, in fact, as if he were a mere confidant, and she were singing a hymn in praise of her beloved.

And thus she spared him any feeling of shame.

But what was to happen now?

It went without saying that this visit must have consequences of some sort. It was her right to demand that he do not, for a second time, take her up and then fling her aside at the convenience of a given hour.

Almost timidly he asked after her thoughts of the future.

"Let's not speak of it. You won't come back, anyhow."

"How can you think. . ."

"Oh, no, you won't come back. And what is there here for you? Do you want to be adored by me? You spoiled gentlemen soon tire of that sort of thing. . . Or would you like to converse with my husband? That wouldn't amuse you. He's a very silent man and his reserve thaws only when he is alone with me. . . But it doesn't matter. . . You have been here. And the memory of this hour will always be dear and precious to me. Now, I have something more in which my soul can take pleasure."

A muffled pain stirred in him. He felt impelled to throw himself at her feet and bury his head in her lap. But he respected the majesty of her happiness.

"And if I myself desired. . ."

That was all he said; all he dared to say. The sudden glory in her face commanded his silence. Under the prudence which his long experience dictated, his mood grew calmer.

But she had understood him.

In silent blessedness, she leaned her head against the wall. Then she whispered, with closed eyes: "It is well that you said no more. I might grow bold and revive hopes that are dead. But if you. . ."

She raised her eyes to his. A complete surrender to his will lay in her glance.

Then she raised her head with a listening gesture.

"My husband," she said, after she had fought

down a slight involuntary fright, and said it with sincere joy.

Three glowing fingers barely touched his. Then she hastened to the door.

"Guess who is here," she called out; "guess!"

On the threshold appeared a sturdy man of middle size and middle age. His round, blonde beard came to a grayish point beneath the chin. His thin cheeks were yellow, but with no unhealthful hue. His quiet, friendly eyes gleamed behind glasses that sat a trifle too far down his nose, so that in speaking his head was slightly thrown back and his lids drawn.

With quiet astonishment he regarded the elegant stranger. Coming nearer, however, he recognised him at once in spite of the twilight, and, a little confused with pleasure, stretched out his hand.

Upon his tired, peaceful features, there was no sign of any sense of strangeness, any desire for an explanation.

Stueckrath realized that toward so simple a nature craft would have been out of place, and simply declared that he had desired to renew an acquaintance which he had always remembered with much pleasure.

"I don't want to speak of myself, Baron," the man replied, "but you probably scarcely realise what pleasure you are giving my wife."

And he nodded down at her who stood beside him, apparently unconcerned except for her wifely joy.

A few friendly words were exchanged. Further speech was really superfluous, since the man's unassailable innocence demanded no caution. But Stueckrath was too much pleased with him to let him feel his insignificance by an immediate departure.

Hence he sat a little longer, told of his latest purchases, and was shamed by the satisfaction with which the man rehearsed the history of his stable.

He did not neglect the courtesy of asking them both to call on him, and took his leave, accompanied by the couple to the door. He could not decide which of the two pressed his hand more warmly.

When in the darkness of the lower hall he looked upward, he saw two faces which gazed after him with genuine feeling.

Out amid the common noises of the street he had the feeling as though he had returned from some far island of alien seas into the wonted current of life.

He shuddered at the thought of what lay before him.

Then he went toward the *Tiergarten*.

A red afterglow eddied amid the trees. In the sky gleamed a harmony of delicate blue tints, shading into green. Great white clouds towered above, but rested upon the redness of the sunset.

The human stream flooded as always between the flickering, starry street-lamps of the *Tiergartenstrasse*. Each man and woman sought to wrest a last hour of radiance from the dying day.

Dreaming, estranged, Stueckrath made his way through the crowd, and hurriedly sought a lonely footpath that disappeared in the darkness of the foliage.

Again for a moment the thought seared him: "Take her and rebuild the structure of your life."

But when he sought to hold the thought and the accompanying emotion, it was gone. Nothing remained but a flat after taste—the dregs of a weary intoxication.

The withered leaves rustled beneath his tread. Beside the path glimmered the leaf-flecked surface of a pool.

"It would be a crime, to be sure," he said to himself, "to shatter the peace of those two poor souls. But, after all, life is made up of such crimes. The life of one is the other's death; one's happiness the other's wretchedness. If only I could be sure that some happiness would result, that the sacrifice of their idyl would bring some profit."

But he had too often had the discouraging and disappointing experience that he had become incapable of any strong and enduring emotion. What had he to offer that woman, who, in a mixture of passion, and naïve unmorality of soul, had thrown herself at his breast? The shallow dregs of a draught, a power to love that had been wasted in sensual trifling—emptiness, weariness, a longing for sensation and a longing for repose. That was all the gift he could bring her.

And how soon would he be satiated!

Any sign of remorse or of fear in her would suffice to make her a burden, even a hated burden!

"Be her good angel," he said to himself, "and let her be." He whistled and the sound was echoed by the trees.

He sought a bench on which to sit down, and lit a cigarette. As the match flared up, he became conscious of the fact that night had fallen.

A great quietude rested upon the dying forest. Like the strains of a beautifully perishing harmony the sound of the world's distant strife floated into this solitude.

Attentively Stueckrath observed the little

point of glowing fire in his hand, from which eddied upward a wreath of fragrant smoke.

"Thank God," he said, "that at least remains —one's cigarette."

Then he arose and wandered thoughtfully onward.

Without knowing how he had come there, he found himself suddenly in front of his mistress's dwelling.

Light shimmered in her windows—the raspberry coloured light of red curtains which loose women delight in.

"Pah!" he said and shuddered.

But, after all, up there a supper table was set for him; there was laughter and society, warmth and a pair of slippers.

He opened the gate.

A chill wind rattled in the twigs of the trees and blew the dead leaves about in conical whirls. They fluttered along like wandering shadows, only to end in some puddle. . .

Autumn. . .

MERRY FOLK

MERRY FOLK

The Christmas tree bent heavily forward. The side which was turned to the wall had been hard to reach, and had hence not been adorned richly enough to keep the equilibrium of the tree against the weighty twigs of the front.

Papa noted this and scolded. "What would Mamma say if she saw that? You know, Brigitta, that Mamma doesn't love carelessness. If the tree falls over, think how ashamed we shall be."

Brigitta flushed fiery red. She clambered up the ladder once more, stretched her arms forth as far as possible, and hung on the other side of the tree all that she could gather. There *had* been very little there. But then one couldn't see. . .

And now the lights could be lit.

"Now we will look through the presents," said Papa. "Which is Mamma's plate?"

Brigitta showed it to him.

This time he was satisfied. "It's a good thing that you've put so much marchpane on it," he said. "You know she always loves to have something to give away." Then he inspected the polished safety lock that lay next to the plate and caressed the hard leaves of the potted palm that shadowed Mamma's place at the Christmas table.

"You have painted the flower vase for her?" he asked.

Brigitta nodded.

"It is exclusively for roses," she said, "and the colours are burned in and will stand any kind of weather."

"What the boys have made for Mamma they can bring her themselves. Have you put down the presents from her?"

Surely she had done so. For Fritz, there was a fishing-net and a ten-bladed knife; for Arthur a turning lathe with foot-power, and in addition a tall toy ship with a golden-haired nymph as figurehead.

"The mermaid will make an impression," said Papa and laughed.

There was something else which Brigitta had on her conscience. She stuck her firm little hands under her apron, which fell straight down over her flat little chest, and tripped up and down on her heels.

"I may as well betray the secret," she said. "Mamma has something for you, too."

Papa was all ear. "What is it?" he asked, and looked over his place at the table, where nothing was noticeable in addition to Brigitta's fancy work.

Brigitta ran to the piano and pulled forth from under it a paper wrapped box, about two feet in height, which seemed singularly light for its size.

When the paper wrappings had fallen aside, a wooden cage appeared, in which sat a stuffed bird that glittered with all the colours of the rainbow. His plumage looked as though the blue of the sky and the gold of the sun had been caught in it.

"A roller!" Papa cried, clapping his hands, and something like joy twitched about his mouth. "And she gives me this rare specimen?"

"Yes," said Brigitta, "it was found last autumn in the throstle springe. The manager kept it for me until now. And because it is so beautiful, and, one might really say, a kind of bird of paradise, therefore Mamma gives it to you."

Papa stroked her blonde hair and again her face flushed.

"So; and now we'll call the boys," he said.

"First let me put away my apron," she cried, loosened the pin and threw the ugly black thing under the piano where the cage had been before.

Now she stood there in her white communion dress, with its blue ribands, and made a charming little grimace.

"You have done quite right," said Papa. "Mamma does not like dark colours. Everything about her is to be bright and gay."

Now the boys were permitted to come in.

They held their beautifully written Christmas poems carefully in their hands and rubbed their sides timidly against the door-posts.

"Come, be cheerful," said Papa. "Do you think your heads will be torn off to-day?"

And then he took them both into his arms and squeezed them a little so that Arthur's poetry was crushed right down the middle.

That was a misfortune, to be sure. But Papa consoled the boy, saying that he would be responsible since it was his fault.

Brueggemann, the long, lean private tutor, now stuck his head in the door, too. He had on his most solemn long coat, nodded sadly like one bidden to a funeral, and sniffed through his nose: "Yes—yes—yes—yes——"

"What are you sighing over so pitiably, you old weeping-willow?" Papa said, laughing. "There are only merry folk here. Isn't it so, Brigitta?"

"Of course that is so," the girl said. "And here, Doctor, is your Christmas plate."

She led him to his place where a little purse of calf's leather peeped modestly out from under the cakes.

"This is your present from Mamma," she continued, handing him a long, dark-covered book. "It is 'The Three Ways to Peace,' which you always admired so much."

The learned gentleman hid a tear of emotion but squinted again at the little pocketbook. This represented the fourth way to peace, for he had old beer debts.

The servants were now ushered in, too. First came Mrs. Poensgen, the housekeeper, who carried in her crooked, scarred hands a little flowerpot with Alpine violets.

"This is for Mamma," she said to Brigitta, who took the pot from her and led her to her own place. There were many good things, among them a brown knitted sweater, such as she had long desired, for in the kitchen an east wind was wont to blow through the cracks.

Mrs. Poensgen saw the sweater as rapidly as Brueggemann had seen the purse. And when Brigitta said: "That is, of course, from Mamma," the old woman was not in the least surprised. For in her fifteen years of service she had discovered that the best things always came from Mamma.

The two boys, in the meantime, were anxious

to ease their consciences and recite their poems. They stood around Papa.

He was busy with the inspectors of the estate, and did not notice them for a moment. Then he became aware of his oversight and took the sheets from their hands, laughing and regretting his neglect. Fritz assumed the proper attitude, and Papa did the same, but when the latter saw the heading of the poem: "To his dear parents at Christmastide," he changed his mind and said: "Let's leave that till later when we are with Mamma."

And so the boys could go on to their places. And as their joy expressed itself at first in a happy silence, Papa stepped up behind them and shook them and said: "Will you be merry, you little scamps? What is Mamma to think if you're not!"

That broke the spell which had held them heretofore. Fritz set his net, and when Arthur discovered a pinnace on his man-of-war, the feeling of immeasurable wealth broke out in jubilation.

But this is the way of the heart. Scarcely had they discovered their own wealth but they turned in desire to that which was not for them.

Arthur had discovered the shiny patent lock that lay between Mamma's plate and his own. It seemed uncertain whether it was for him or her. He felt pretty well assured that it was not for him; on the other hand, he couldn't imagine what use she could put it to. Furthermore, he was interested in it, since it was made upon a certain model. It is not for nothing that one is an engineer with all one's heart and mind.

Now, Fritz tried to give an expert opinion, too. He considered it a combination Chubb lock. Of course that was utter nonsense. But then Fritz would sometimes talk at random.

However that may be, this lock was undoubtedly the finest thing of all. And when one turned the key in it, it gave forth a soft, slow, echoing tone, as though a harp-playing spirit sat in its steel body.

But Papa came and put an end to their delight.

"What are you thinking of, you rascals?" he said in jesting reproach. "Instead of giving poor Mamma something for Christmas, you want to take the little that she has."

At that they were mightily ashamed. And Arthur said that of course they had something for Mamma, only they had left it in the hall, so that they could take it at once when they went to her.

"Get it in," said Papa, "in order that her place may not look so meager."

They ran out and came back with their presents.

Fritz had carved a flower-pot holder. It consisted of six parts, which dove-tailed delicately into each other. But that was nothing compared to Arthur's ventilation window, which was woven of horse hair.

Papa was delighted. "Now we needn't be ashamed to be seen," he said. Then, too, he explained to them the mechanism of the lock, and told them that its purpose was to guard dear Mamma's flowers better. For recently some of her favourite roses had been stolen and the only way to account for it was that some one had a pass key.

"So, and now we'll go to her at last," he concluded. "We have kept her waiting long. And we will be happy with her, for happiness is the great thing, as Mamma says. . . Get us the key, Brigitta, to the gate and the chapel."

And Brigitta got the key to the gate and the chapel.

THEA

THEA

A Phantasy over the Samovar

I.

SHE is a faery and yet she is none. . . .
But she is my faery surely.

She has appeared to me only in a few moments of life when I least expected her.

And when I desired to hold her, she vanished.

Yet has she often dwelt near me. I felt her in the breath of winter winds sweeping over sunny fields of snow; I breathed her presence in the morning frost that clung, glittering, to my beard; I saw the shadow of her gigantic form glide over the smoky darkness of heaven which hung with the quietude of hopelessness over the dull white fields; I heard the whispering of her voice in the depths of the shining tea urn surrounded by a dancing wreath of spirit flames.

But I must tell the story of those few times when she stood bodily before me—changed of form and yet the same—my fate, my future as it should have been and was not, my fear and my trust, my good and my evil star.

II.

IT was many, many years ago on a late evening near Epiphany.

Without whirled the snow. The flakes came fluttering to the windows like endless swarms of moths. Silently they touched the panes and then glided straight down to earth as though they had broken their wings in the impact.

The lamp, old and bad for the eyes, stood on the table with its polished brass foot and its raveled green cloth shade. The oil in the tank gurgled dutifully. Black fragments gathered on the wick, which looked like a stake over which a few last flames keep watch.

Yonder in the shabby upholstered chair my mother had fallen into a doze. Her knitting had dropped from her hands and lay on the flower-patterned apron. The wool-thread cut a deep furrow in the skin of her rough forefinger. One of the needles swung behind her ear.

The samovar with its bellied body and its shining chimney stood on a side table. From time to time a small, pale-blue cloud of steam whirled upward, and a gentle odour of burning charcoal tickled my nostrils.

Before me on the table lay open Sallust's "Catilinarian Conspiracy!" But what did I care for Sallust? Yonder on the book shelf, laughing and alluring in its gorgeous cover stood the first novel that I ever read—"The Adventures of Baron Muenchausen!"

Ten pages more to construe. Then I was free. I buried my hands deep into my breeches pockets, for I was cold. Only ten pages more.

Yearningly I stared at my friend.

And behold, the bookbinder's crude ornamentation—ungraceful arabesques of vine leaves which wreathe about broken columns, a rising sun caught in a spider's web of rays—all that configuration begins to spread and distend until it fills the room. The vine leaves tremble in a morning wind; a soft blowing shakes the columns, and higher and higher mounts the sun. Like a dance of flickering torches his rays shoot to and fro, his glistening arms are outstretched as though they would grasp the world and pull it to the burning bosom of the sun. And a great roaring arises in the air, muffled and deep as distant organ strains. It rises to the blare of trumpets, it quivers with the clash of cymbals.

Then the body of the sun bursts open. A bluish, phosphorescent flame hisses forth. Upon this flame stands erect in fluttering *chiton* a woman, fair and golden haired, swan's wings at her shoulders, a harp held in her hand.

She sees me and her face is full of laughter. Her laughter sounds simple, childlike, arch. And surely, it is a child's mouth from which it issues. The innocent blue eyes look at me in mad challenge. The firm cheeks glow with the delight of life. Heavens! What is this child's head doing on that body? She throws the harp upon the clouds, sits down on the strings, scratches her little nose swiftly with her left wing and calls out to me: "Come, slide with me!"

I stare at her open-mouthed. Then I gather all my courage and stammer: "Who are you?"

"My name is Thea," she giggles.

"But *who* are you?" I ask again.

"Who? Nonsense. Come, pull me! But no; you can't fly. I'll pull you. That will go quicker."

And she arises. Heavens! What a form! Magnificently the hips curve over the fallen girdle; in how noble a line are throat and bosom married. No sculptor can achieve the like.

With her slender fingers she grasps the blue, embroidered riband that is attached to the neck of the harp. She grasps it with the gesture of one who is about to pull a sleigh.

"Come," she cries again.

I dare not understand her. Awkwardly I crouch on the strings.

"I might break them," I venture.

"You little shaver," she laughs. "Do you know how light you are? And now, hold fast!"

I have scarcely time to grasp the golden frame with both hands. I hear a mighty rustling in front of me. The mighty wings unfold. My sleigh floats and billows in the air. Forward and upward goes the roaring flight.

Far, far beneath me lies the paternal hut. Scarcely does its light penetrate to my height. Gusts of snow whirl about my forehead. Next moment the light is wholly lost. Dawn breaks through the night. A warm wind meets us and blows upon the strings so that they tremble gently and lament like a sleeping child whose soul is troubled by a dream of loneliness.

"Look down!" cried my faery, turning her laughing little head toward me.

Bathed in the glow of spring I see an endless carpet of woods and hills, fields and lakes spread out below me. The landscape gleams with a greenish silveriness. My glance can scarcely endure the richness of the miracle.

"But it has become spring," I say trembling.

"Would you like to go down?" she asks.

"Yes, yes."

At once we glide downward.

"Guess what that is!" she says.

An old, half-ruined castle rears its granite walls before me. . . . A thousand year old ivy wreathes about its gables. . . . Black and white swallows dart about the roofs. . . . All about arises a thicket of hawthorn in full bloom. . . . Wild roses emerge from the darkness, innocently agleam like children's eyes. A sleepy tree bends its boughs above them.

There is life at the edge of the ancient terrace where broad-leaved clover grows in the broken urns. A girlish form, slender and lithe, swinging a great, old-fashioned straw hat, having a shawl wound crosswise over throat and waist, has stepped forth from the decaying old gate. She carries a little white bundle under her arm, and looks tentatively to the right and to the left as one who is about to go on a journey.

"Look at her," says my friend.

The scales fall from my eyes.

"That is Lisbeth," I cried out in delight, "who is going to the mayor's farm."

Scarcely have I mentioned that farm but a fragrance of roasting meat rises up to me. Clouds of smoke roll toward me, dim flames quiver up from it. There is a sound of roasting and frying and the seething fat spurts high. No wonder; there's going to be a wedding.

"Would you like to see the executioner's sword?" my friend asks.

A mysterious shudder runs down my limbs.

"I'd like to well enough," I say fearfully.

A rustle, a soft metallic rattle—and we are in a small, bare chamber. . . . Now it is night again and the moonlight dances on the rough board walls.

"Look there," whispers my friend and points to a plump old chest.

Her laughing face has grown severe and solemn. Her body seems to have grown. Noble and lordly as a judge she stands before me.

I stretch my neck; I peer at the chest.

There it lies, gleaming and silent, the old sword. A beam of moonlight glides along the old blade, drawing a long, straight line. But what do those dark spots mean which have eaten hollows into the metal?

"That is blood," says my friend and crosses her arms upon her breast.

I shiver but my eyes seem to have grown fast to the terrible image.

"Come," says Thea.

"I can't."

"Do you want it?"

"What? The sword?"

She nods.

"But may you give it away? Does it belong to you?"

"I may do anything. Everything belongs to me."

A horror grips me with its iron fist. "Give it to me!" I cry shuddering.

The iron lightening gleams up and it lies cold and moist in my arms. It seems to me as though the blood upon it began to flow afresh.

My arms feel dead, the sword falls from them and sinks upon the strings. These begin to moan and sing. Their sounds are almost like cries of pain.

"Take care," cries my friend. "The sword may rend the strings; it is heavier than you."

We fly out into the moonlit night. But our flight is slower than before. My friend breathes hard and the harp swings to and fro like a paper kite in danger of fluttering to earth.

But I pay no attention to all that. Something very amusing captures my senses.

Something has become alive in the moon which floats, a golden disc, amid the clouds. Something black and cleft twitches to and fro on her nether side. I look more sharply and discover a pair of old riding-boots in which stick two long, lean legs. The leather on the inner side of the boots is old and worn and glimmers with a dull discoloured light.

"Since when does the moon march on legs through the world?" I ask myself and begin to laugh. And suddenly I see something black on the upper side of the moon—something that wags funnily up and down. I strain my eyes and recognise my old friend Muenchausen's phantastic beard and moustache. He has grasped the edges of the moon's disc with his long lean fingers and laughs, laughs.

"I want to go there," I call to my friend.

She turns around. Her childlike face has now become grave and madonna like. She seems to have aged by years. Her words echo in my ear like the sounds of broken chimes.

"He who carries the sword cannot mount to the moon."

My boyish stubbornness revolts. "But I want to get to my friend Muenchausen."

"He who carries the sword has no friend."

I jump up and tug at the guiding riband. The harp capsises. . . . I fall into emptiness . . . the sword above me . . . it penetrates my body . . . I fall . . . I fall. . . .

"Yes, yes," says my mother, "why do you call so fearfully? I am awake."

Calmly she took the knitting-needle from behind her ear, stuck it into the wool and wrapped the unfinished stocking about it.

III.

Six years passed. Then Thea met me again. She had been gracious enough to leave her home in the island valley of Avilion, to play the soubrette parts in the theatre of the university town in which I was fencing and drinking for the improvement of my mind.

Upon her little red shoes she tripped across the stage. She let her abbreviated skirts wave in the boldest curves. She wore black silk stockings which flowed about her delicate ankles in ravishing lines and disappeared all too soon, just above the knee, under the hem of her skirt. She plaited herself two thick braids of hair the blue ribands of which she loved to chew when the modesty that belonged to her part overwhelmed her. She sucked her thumb, she stuck out her tongue, she squeaked and shrieked and turned up her little nose. And, oh, how she laughed. It was that sweet, sophisticated, vicious soubrette laughter which begins with the musical scale and ends in a long coo.

Show me the man among us whom she cannot madden into love with all the traditional tricks of her trade. Show me the student who did not

keep glowing odes deep-buried in his lecture
notes—deep-buried as the gigantic grief of some
heroic soul. . . .

And one afternoon she appeared at the skat-
ing rink. She wore a gleaming plush jacket
trimmed with sealskin, and a fur cap which sat
jauntily over her left ear. The hoar frost clung
like diamond dust to the reddish hair that framed
her cheeks, and her pink little nose sniffed up the
cold air.

After she had made a scene with the attendant
who helped her on with her shoes, during which
such expressions as "idiot," had escaped her
sweet lips, she began to skate. A child, just
learning to walk, could have done better.

We foolish boys stood about and stared at her.

The desire to help her waxed in us to the intensity of madness. But when pouting she
stretched out her helpless arms at us, we recoiled
as before an evil spirit. Not one of us found
the courage simply to accept the superhuman
bliss for which he had been hungering by day
and night for months.

Then suddenly—at an awful curve—she
caught her foot, stumbled, wavered first forward
and then backward and finally fell into the arms
of the most diffident and impassioned of us all.

And that was I.

Yes, that was I.

To this day my fists are clenched with rage at the thought that it might have been another.

Among those who remained behind as I led her away in triumph there was not one who could not have slain me with a calm smile.

Under the impact of the words which she wasted upon my unworthy self, I cast down my eyes, smiling and blushing. Then I taught her how to set her feet and showed off my boldest manœuvres. I also told her that I was a student in my second semester and that it was my ambition to be a poet.

"Isn't that sweet?" she exclaimed. "I suppose you write poetry already?"

I certainly did. I even had a play in hand which treated of the fate of the troubadour Bernard de Ventadours in rhymeless, irregular verse.

"Is there a part for me in it?" she asked.

"No," I answered, "but it doesn't matter. I'll put one in."

"Oh, how sweet that is of you!" she cried. "And do you know? You must read me the play. I can help you with my practical knowledge of the stage."

A wave of bliss under which I almost suffocated, poured itself out over me.

"I have also written poems—to you!" I stammered. The wave carried me away.

"Think of that," she said quite kindly instead of boxing my ears. "You must send them to me."

"Surely." . . .

And then I escorted her to the door while my friends followed us at a seemly distance like a pack of wolves.

The first half of the night I passed ogling beneath her window; the second half at my table, for I wanted to enrich the packet to be sent her by some further lyric pearls. At the peep of dawn I pushed the envelope, tight as a drum with its contents, into the pillar box and went to cool my burning head on the ramparts.

On that very afternoon came a violet-tinted little letter which had an exceedingly heady fragrance and bore instead of a seal a golden lyre transfixed by a torch. It contained the following lines:

"DEAR POET:

"Your verses aren't half bad; only too fiery. I'm really in a hurry to hear your play. My old chaperone is going out this evening. I will be at home alone and will, therefore, be bored. So come to tea at seven. But you must give me your word of honour that you do not give away this secret. Otherwise I won't care for you the least bit.

　　　　"Your　　　　　　　　THEA."

Thus did she write, I swear it—she, my faery, my Muse, my Egeria, she to whom I desired to look up in adoration to the last drawing of my breath.

Swiftly I revised and corrected and recited several scenes of my play. I struck out half a dozen superfluous characters and added a dozen others.

At half past six I set out on my way. A thick, icy fog lay in the air. Each person that I met was covered by a cloud of icy breath.

I stopped in front of a florist's shop.

All the treasures of May lay exposed there on little terraces of black velvet. There were whole beds of violets and bushes of snow-drops. There was a great bunch of long-stemmed roses, carelessly held together by a riband of violet silk.

I sighed deeply. I knew why I sighed.

And then I counted my available capital: Eight marks and seventy pfennigs. Seven beer checks I have in addition. But these, alas, are good only at my inn—for fifteen pfennigs worth of beer a piece.

At last I take courage and step into the shop.

"What is the price of that bunch of roses?" I whisper. I dare not speak aloud, partly by reason of the great secret and partly through diffidence.

"Ten marks," says the fat old saleswoman.
She lets the palm leaves that lie on her lap slip
easily into an earthen vessel and proceeds to the
window to fetch the roses.

I am pale with fright. My first thought is:
Run to the inn and try to exchange your checks
for cash. You can't borrow anything two days
before the first of the month.

Suddenly I hear the booming of the tower
clock.

"Can't I get it a little cheaper?" I ask half-
throttled.

"Well, did you ever?" she says, obviously
hurt. "There are ten roses in the bunch; they
cost a mark a piece at this time. We throw in
the riband."

I am disconsolate and am about to leave
the shop. But the old saleswoman who
knows her customers and has perceived the
tale of love lurking under my whispering
and my hesitation, feels a human sympathy.

"You might have a few roses taken out," she
says. "How much would you care to expend,
young man?"

"Eight marks and seventy pfennigs," I am
about to answer in my folly. Fortunately it occurs to me that I must keep out a tip for her
maid. The ladies of the theatre always have

maids. And I might leave late. "Seven marks,"
I answer therefore.

With quiet dignity the woman extracts *four*
roses from my bunch and I am too humble and
intimidated to protest.

But my bunch is still rich and full and I am
consoled to think that a wooing prince cannot do
better.

Five minutes past seven I stand before her
door.

Need I say that my breath gives out, that I
dare not knock, that the flowers nearly fall from
my nerveless hand? All that is a matter of
course to anyone who has ever, in his youth, had
dealings with faeries of Thea's stamp.

It is a problem to me to this day how I finally
did get into her room. But already I see her
hastening toward me with laughter and bury-
ing her face in the roses.

"O you spendthrift!" she cries and tears the
flowers from my hand in order to pirouette with
them before the mirror. And then she assumes
a solemn expression and takes me by a coat but-
ton, draws me nearer and says: "So, and now
you may kiss me as a reward."

I hear and cannot grasp my bliss. My heart
seems to struggle out at my throat, but hard before me bloom her lips. I am brave and kiss
her.

"Oh," she says, "your beard is full of snow."

"My beard! Hear it, ye gods! Seriously and with dignity she speaks of my beard."

A turbid sense of being a kind of Don Juan or Lovelace arises in me. My self-consciousness assumes heroic dimensions, and I begin to regard what is to come with a kind of dæmonic humour.

The mist that has hitherto blurred my vision departs. I am able to look about me and to recognise the place where I am.

To be sure, that is a new and unsuspected world—from the rosy silken gauze over the toilet mirror that hangs from the beaks of two floating doves, to the row of exquisite little laced boots that stands in the opposite corner. From the candy boxes of satin, gold, glass, saffron, ivory, porcelain and olive wood which adorn the dresser to the edges of white billowy skirts which hang in the next room but have been caught in the door—I see nothing but miracles, miracles.

A maddening fragrance assaults my senses, the same which her note exhaled. But now that fragrance streams from her delicate, graceful form in its princess gown of pale yellow with red bows. She dances and flutters about the room with so mysterious and elf-like a grace as though she were playing Puck in the "Midsummer

Night's Dream," the part in which she first en-thralled my heart.

Ah, yes, she meant to get tea.

"Well, why do you stand there so helplessly, you horrid creature? Come! Here is a table-cloth, here are knives and forks. I'll light the spirit lamp in the meantime."

And she slips by me not without having admin-istered a playful tap to my cheek and vanishes in the dark room of mystery.

I am about to follow her, but out of the dark-ness I hear a laughing voice: "Will you stay where you are, Mr. Curiosity?"

And so I stand still on the threshold and lay my head against those billowy skirts. They are fresh and cool and ease my burning forehead.

Immediately thereafter I see the light of a match flare up in the darkness, which for a mo-ment sharply illuminates the folds of her dress and is then extinguished. Only a feeble, bluish flame remains. This flame plays about a pol-ished little urn and illuminates dimly the secrets of the forbidden sanctuary. I see bright bil-lowy garments, bunches of flowers and wreaths of leaves, with long, silken, shimmering bands—and suddenly the flame flares high. . . .

"Now I've spilt the alcohol," I hear the voice of my friend. But her laughter is full of sar-castic arrogance. "Ah, that'll be a play of fire!"

Higher and higher mount the flames.

"Come, jump into it!" she cries out to me, and instead of quenching the flame she pours forth more alcohol into the furious conflagration.

"For heaven's sake!" I cry out.

"Do you know now who I am?" she giggles. "I'm a witch!"

With jubilant screams she loosens her hair of reddish gold which now falls about her with a flaming glory. She shows me her white sharp teeth and with a sudden swift movement she springs into the flame which hisses to the very ceiling and clothes the chamber in a garb of fire.

I try to call for help, but my throat is tied, my breath stops. I am throttled by smoke and flames.

Once more I hear her elfin laughter, but now it comes to me from subterranean depths. The earth has opened; new flames arise and stretch forth fiery arms toward me.

A voice cries from the fires: "Come! Come!" And the voice is like the sound of bells. Then suddenly the night enfolds me.

The witchery has fled. Badly torn and scarred I find myself again on the street. Next to me on the ground lies my play.

"Did you not mean to read that to some one?" I ask myself.

A warm and gentle air caresses my fevered face. A blossoming lilac bush inclines its boughs above me and from afar, there where the dawn is about to appear, I hear the clear trilling of larks.

I dream no longer. . . . But the spring has come. . . .

IV.

AND again the years pass by.

It was on an evening during the carnival season and the world, that is, the world that begins with the baron and ends with the stockjobber, floated upon waves of pleasure as bubbles of fat float on the surface of soup.

Whoever did not wallow in the mire was sarcastically said not to be able to sustain himself on his legs.

There were those among my friends who had not gone to bed till morning for thirty days. Some of them slept only to the strains of a world-famous virtuoso; others only in the cabs that took them from dinner to supper.

Whenever three of them met, one complained of shattered nerves, the second of catarrh of the stomach, the third of both.

That was the pace of our amusement.

Of mine, too.

It was nearly one' o'clock in the morning. I sat in a *café,* that famous *café* which unacknowleged geniuses affirm to be the very centre of all intellectual life. No spot on earth is said to have so fruitful an effect upon one's genius.

Yet, strangely enough, however eager for inspiration I might lounge about its red upholstery, however ardently aglow for inspiration I might drink expensive champagnes there, yet the supreme, immense, all-liberating thought did not come.

Nor would that thought come to me to-day. Less than ever, in fact. Red circles danced before my eyes and in my veins hammered the throbs of fever. It wasn't surprising. For I, too, could scarcely remember to have slept recently. It is an effort to raise my lids. The hand that would stroke the hair with the gesture of genius—alas, how thin the hair is getting—sinks down in nerveless weakness.

But I may not go home. Mrs. Elsbeth—we bachelors call her so when her husband is not by—Mrs. Elsbeth has ordered me to be here. . . . She intended to drop in at midnight on her return from dinner with her husband. The purpose of her coming is to discuss with me the surprises which I am to think up for her magic festival.

She is exacting enough, the sweet little woman, but the world has it that I love her. And in order to let the world be in the right a man is not averse to making a fool of herself.

The stream of humanity eddies about me. Like endless chains rotating in different directions, thus seem the two lines of those who enter and those who depart. There are dandies in coquettish furs, their silk hats low on their foreheads, their canes held vertically in their pockets. There are fashionable ladies in white silk opera cloaks set with ermine, their eyes peering from behind Spanish veils in proud curiosity. And all are illuminated by the spirit of festivity.

Also one sees shop-girls, dragged here by some chance admirer. They wear brownish cloaks, ornamented with knots—the kind that looks worn the day it is taken from the shop. And there are ladies of that species whom one calls "ladies" only between quotation marks. These wear gigantic picture hats trimmed with rhinestones. The hems of their dresses are torn and flecked with last season's mud. There are students who desire to be intoxicated through the lust of the eye; artists who desire to regain a lost sobriety of vision; journalists who find stuff for leader copy in the blue despatches that are posted here; Bohemians and loungers of every station, typical of every degree of sham dignity and equally sham depravity. They all intermingle in mani-coloured waves. It is the mad masque of the metropolis. . . .

A friend comes up to me, one of the three hundred bosom friends with whom I am wont to swap shady stories. He is pallid with sleep-

lessness, deep horizontal lines furrow his forehead, his brows are convulsively drawn. So we
all look . . .

"Look here," he says, "you weren't at the
Meyers' yesterday."

"I was invited elsewhere."

"Where?"

I've got to think a minute before I can remember the name. We all suffer from weakness in the head.

"Aha," he cries. "I'm told it was swell.
Magnificent women . . . and that fellow
. . . er . . . thought reader and what's
her name . . . yes . . . the Sembrich
. . . swell . . . you must introduce me
there some day. . . ."

Stretching his legs he sinks down at my side
on the sofa.

Silence. My bosom friend and I have exhausted the common stock of interests.

He has lit a cigarette and is busy catching the
white clouds which he blows from his nose with
his mouth. This employment seems to satisfy
his intellect wholly.

I, for my part, stare at the ceiling. There the
golden bodies of snakes wind themselves in mad
arabesques through chains of roses. The pre-
tentious luxury offends my eye. I look farther,
past the candelabrum of crystal which reflects

sharp rainbow tints over all, past the painted
columns whose shafts end in lily leaves as some
torturing spear does in flesh.

My glance stops yonder on the wall where a
series of fresco pictures has been painted.

The forms of an age that was drunk with
beauty look down on me in their victorious calm.
They are steeped in the glow of a southern
heaven. The rigid splendour of the marble walls
is contrasted with the magnificent flow of long
garments.

It is a Roman supper. Rose-crowned men
lean upon Indian cushions, holding golden beak-
ers in their right hands. Women in yielding
nakedness cower at their feet. Through the open
door streams in a Bacchic procession with fauns
and panthers, the drunken Pan in its midst.
Brown-skinned slaves with leopard skins about
their loins make mad music. Among them is one
who at once makes me forget the tumult. She
leans her firm, naked body surreptitiously against
the pillar. Her form is contracted with weariness. Thoughtlessly and with tired lips she blows
the *tibia* which her nerveless hands threaten to
drop. Her cheeks are yellow and fallen in, her
eyes are glassy, but upon her forehead are seen
the folds of lordship and about her mouth
wreaths a stony smile of irony.

Who is she? Whence does she come? I ask
myself. But I feel a dull thud against my
shoulder. My bosom friend has fallen asleep
and is using me as a pillow.

"Look here, you!" I call out to him, for I
have for the moment forgotten his name. "Go
home and go to bed."

He starts up and gazes at me with swimming
eyes.

"Do you mean me?" he stutters. "That's a
good joke." And next moment he begins to
snore.

I hide him as well as possible with my broad
back and bend down over the glittering samovar
before me. The fragrant steam prickles my
nose.

It is time that the little woman turn up if I
am to amuse her guests.

I think of the brown-skinned woman yonder
in the painting.

I open my eyes. Merciful heaven! What is
that?

For the woman stands erect now in all the firm
magnificence of her young limbs, presses her
clenched fists against her forehead and stares
down at me with glowing eyes.

And suddenly she hurls the flutes from her in
a long curve and cries with piercing voice: "No
more . . . I will play no more!"

It is the voice of a slave at the moment of liberation.

"For heaven's sake, woman!" I cry. "What are you doing? You will be slain; you will be thrown to the wild beasts!"

She points about her with a gesture that is full of disgust and contempt.

Then I see what she means. All that company has fallen asleep. The men lie back with open mouths, the goblets still in their hands. Golden cascades of wine fall glittering upon the marble. The women writhe in these pools of wine. But even in the intoxication of their dreams they try to guard their elaborate hair dress. The whole mad band, musicians and animals, lies there with limbs dissolved, panting for air, overwhelmed by heavy sleep.

"The way is free!" cries the flute player jubilantly and buries her twitching fingers into the flesh of her breasts. "What is there to hinder my flight?"

"Whither do you flee, mad woman?" I ask.

A gleam of dreamy ecstasy glides over her grief-worn face which seems to flush and grow softer of outline.

"Home—to freedom," she whispers down to me and her eyes burn.

"Where is your home?"

"In the desert," she cries. "Here I play for

their dances; there I am queen. My name is
Thea and it is resonant through storms. They
chained me with golden chains; they lured me
with golden speeches until I left my people and
followed them to their prison that is corroded
with lust. . . . Ah, if you knew with my
knowledge, you would not sit here either. . . .
But the slave of the moment knows not liberty."

"I have known it," I say drearily and let my
chin sink upon the table.

"And you are here?"

Contemptuously she turns her back to me.

"Take me with you, Thea," I cry, "take me
with you to freedom."

"Can you still endure it."

"I will endure the glory of freedom or die of
it."

"Then come."

A brown arm that seems endless stretches
down to me. An iron grasp lifts me upward.
Noise and lights dislimn in the distance.

Our way lies through great, empty, pillared
halls which curve above us like twilit cathedrals.
Great stairs follow which fall into black depths
like waterfalls of stone. Thence issues a mist,
green with silvery edges. . . .

A dizziness seizes me as I strive to look downward.

I have a presentiment of something formless,

limitless. A vague awe and terror fill me. I tremble and draw back but an alien hand constrains me.

We wander along a moonlit street. To the right and left extend pallid plains from which dark cypress trees arise, straight as candles.

It is all wide and desolate like those halls.

In the far distance arise sounds like half smothered cries of the dying, but they grow to music.

Shrill jubilation echoes between the sounds and it too grows to music.

But this music is none other than the roaring of the storm which lashes us on when we dare to faint.

And we wander, wander . . . days, weeks, months. Who knows how long?

Night and day are alike. We do not rest; nor speak.

The road is far behind us. We wander upon trackless wastes.

Stonier grows the way, an eternal up and down over cliffs and through chasms. . . . The edges of the weathered stones become steps for our feet. Breathlessly we climb the peaks. Beyond them we clatter into new abysms.

My feet bleed. My limbs jerk numbly like those of a jumping-jack. An earthy taste is on my lips.

I have long lost all sense of progress. One cliff is like another in its jagged nakedness; one abysm dark and empty as another. Perhaps I wander in a circle. Perhaps this brown hand is leading me wildly astray, this hand whose grasp has penetrated my flesh, and has grown into it like the fetter of a slave.

Suddenly I am alone.

I do not know how it came to pass.

I drag myself to a peak and look about me.

There spreads in the crimson glow of dawn the endless, limitless rocky desert—an ocean turned to stone.

Jagged walls tower in eternal monotony into the immeasurable distance which is hid from me by no merciful mist. Out of invisible abysms arise sharp peaks. A storm from the south lashes their flanks from which the cracked stone fragments roll to become the foundations of new walls.

The sun, hard and sharp as a merciless eye, arises slowly in this parched sky and spreads its cloak of fire over this dead world.

The stone upon which I sit begins to glow.

The storm drives splinters of stone into my flesh. A fiery stream of dust mounts toward me. Madness descends upon me like a fiery canopy.

Shall I wander on? Shall I die?

I wander on, for I am too weary to die.

At last, far off, on a ledge of rock, I see the figure of a man.

Like a black spot it interrupts this sea of light in which the very shadows have become a crimson glow.

An unspeakable yearning after this man fills my soul. For his steps are secure. His feet are scarcely lifted, yet quietly does he fare down the chasms and up the heights. I want to rush to meet him but a great numbness holds me back.

He comes nearer and nearer.

I see a pallid, bearded countenance with high cheekbones, and emaciated cheeks. . . . The mouth, delicate and gentle as a girl's, is drawn in a quiet smile. A bitterness that has grown into love, into renunciation, even into joy, shines in this smile.

And at the sight of it I feel warm and free.

And then I see his eye which is round and sharp as though open through the watches of many nights. With moveless clearness of vision he measures the distances, and is careless of the way which his foot finds without groping. In this look lies a dreaming glow which turns to waking coldness.

A tremour of reverence seizes my body.

And now I know who this man is who fares through the desert in solitary thought, and to whom horror has shown the way to peace.

He looks past me! How could it be different?

I dare not call to him. Movelessly I stare after him until his form has vanished in the guise of a black speck behind the burning cliffs.

Then I wander farther . . . and farther . . . and farther. . . .

It was on a grayish yellow day of autumn that I sat again after an interval on the upholstery of the famous *café*. I looked gratefully up at the brown slave-girl in the picture who blew upon her flutes as sleepily and dully as ever. I had come to see her.

I start for I feel a tap on my shoulder.

In brick-red gloves, his silk-hat over his forehead, a little more tired and world-worn than ever, that bosom friend whose name I have now definitely forgotten stood before me.

"Where the devil have you been all this time?" he asks.

"Somewhere," I answer laughing. "In the desert." . . .

"Gee! What were you looking for there?"

"Myself." . . .

V.

AND ever swifter grows the beat of time's wing. My breath can no longer keep the same pace.

Thoughtless enjoyment of life has long yielded to a life and death struggle.

And I am conquered.

Wretchedness and want have robbed me of my grasping courage and of my laughing defiance. The body is sick and the soul droops its wings.

Midnight approaches. The smoky lamp burns more dimly and outside on the streets life begins to die out. Only from time to time the snow crunches and groans under the hurrying foot of some belated and freezing passer-by. The reflection of the gas lamps rests upon the frozen windows as though a yellow veil had been drawn before them.

In the room hovers a dull heat which weighs upon my brain and even amid shivering wrings the sweat from my pores.

I had the fire started again toward night for I was cold.

Now I am no longer cold.

"Take care of yourself," my friend the doctor said to me, "you have worked yourself to pieces and must rest."

"Rest, rest"—the word sounds like a gnome's irony from all the corners of my room, for my work is heaping up on all sides and threatens to smother me.

"Work! Work!" This is the voice of conscience. It is like the voice of a brutal waggoner that would urge a dead ass on to new efforts.

My paper is in its place. For hours I have sat and stared at it brooding. It is still empty.

A disagreeably sweetish odour which arises impudently to my nose makes me start.

There stands the pitcher of herb tea which my landlady brought in at bedtime.

The dear woman.

"Man must sweat," she had declared. "If the whole man gets into a sweat then the evil humours are exuded, and the healthy sap gets a chance to circulate until one is full of it."

And saying that she wiped her greasy lips for she likes to eat a piece of rye bread with goose grease before going to bed.

Irritatedly I push the little pitcher aside, but its grayish green steam whirls only the more pertinaciously about me. The clouds assume strange forms, which tower over each other and whirl into each other like the phantoms over a witch's cauldron.

And at last the fumes combine into a human form, at first misty and without outlines but gradually becoming more sharply defined.

Gray, gray, gray. An aged woman. So she seems, for she creeps along by the help of a crutch. But over her face is a veil which falls to the ground over her arms like the folded wings of a bat.

I begin to laugh, for spirits have long ceased to inspire me with reverence.

"Is your name by any chance Thea, O lovely being?" I ask.

"My name is Thea," she answers and her voice is weary, gentle and a little hoarse. A caressing shimmer as of faintly blue velvet, an insinuating fragrance as of dying mignonette—both lie in this voice. The voice fills my heart. But I won't be taken in, least of all by some trite ghost which is in the end only a vision of one's own sick brain.

"It seems that the years have not changed you for the better, charming Thea," I say and point sarcastically to the crutch.

"My wings are broken and I am withered like yourself."

I laugh aloud.

"So that is the meaning of this honoured apparition! A mirror of myself—spirit of ruin—a symbolic poem on the course of my ideas. Pshaw! I know that trick. Every brainless Christmas poet knows it, too. You must come with a more powerful charm, O Thea, spirit of the herb tea! Good-bye. My time is too precious to be wasted by allegories."

"What have you to do that is so important?" she asks, and I seem to see the gleam of her eyes behind the folds of the veil, whether in laughter or in grief I cannot tell.

"If I have nothing more to do, I must die," I answer and feel with joy how my defiance steels itself in these words.

"And that seems important to you?"

"Moderately so."

"Important to whom?"

"To myself, I should think, if to no one else."

"And your creditor—the world?"

That was the last straw. "The world, oh, yes, the world. And what, pray, do I owe it?"

"Love."

"Love? To that harlot? Because it sucked the fire from my veins and poured poison therein instead? Behold me here—wrecked, broken, a plaything of any wave. That is what the world has made of me!"

"That is what you have made of yourself!

. . . The world came to you as a smiling
guide. . . . With gentle finger it touched
your shoulder and desired you to follow. But
you were stubborn. You went your own way in
dark and lonely caverns where the laughing music
of the fight that sounds from above becomes a
discordant thunder. You were meant to be
wise and merry; you became dull and morose."

"Very well; if that is what I became, at least
the grave will release me from my condition."

"Test yourself thoroughly."

"What is the use of that now? Life has crip-
pled me. . . . What of joy it has to offer
becomes torture to me. . . . I am cut loose
from all the kindly bonds that bind man to man.
. . . I cannot bear hatred, neither can I bear
love. . . . I tremble at a thousand dangers
that have never threatened and will never
threaten me. A very straw has become a cliff
to me against which I founder and against which
my weary limbs are dashed in pieces. . . .
And this is the worst of all. My vision sees
clearly that it is but a straw before which my
strength writhes in the dust. . . . You have
come at the right time, Thea. Perhaps you carry
in the folds of your robe some little potion that
will help me to hurry across the verge."

Again I see a gleam behind the veil—a smiling
salutation from some far land where the sun is

still shining. And my heart seems about to burst under that gleam. But I control myself and continue to gaze at her with bitter defiance.

"It needs no potion," she says and raises her right hand. I have never seen such a hand. . . . It seem to be without bones, formed of the petals of flowers. The hand might seem deformed, dried and yet swollen as with disease, were it not so delicate, so radiant, so lily-like. An unspeakable yearning for this poor, sick hand overcomes me. I want to fall on my knees before it and press my lips to it in adoration. But already the hand lays itself softly upon my hair. Gentle and cool as a flake of snow it rests there. But from moment to moment it waxes heavier until the weight of mountains seems to lie upon my head. I can bear the pressure no longer. I sink . . . I sink . . . the earth opens . . . Darkness is all about me. . . .

Recovering consciousness, I find myself lying in a bed surrounded by impenetrable night.

"One of my stupid dreams," I say to myself and grope for the matches on my bedside table to see the time. . . . But my hand strikes hard against a board that rises diagonally at my shoulder. I grope farther and discover that my couch is surrounded by a cloak of wood. And that cloak is so narrow, so narrow that I can scarcely raise my head a few inches without knocking against it.

"Perhaps I am buried," I say to myself. "Then indeed my wish would have fulfilled itself promptly."

A fresh softly prickling scent of flowers, as of heather and roses, floats to me.

"Aha," I say to myself, "the odour of the funeral flowers. My favourites have been chosen. That was kind of people." And, as I turn my head the cups of flowers nestle soft and cool against my cheek.

"You are buried amid roses," I say to myself, "as you always desired. And then I touch my breast to discover what gift has been placed upon my heart. My fingers touch hard, jagged leaves.

"What is that?" I ask myself in surprise. And then I laugh shrilly. It is a wreath of laurel leaves which has been pressed with its rough, woodlike leaves between my body and the coffin lid.

"Now you have everything that you so ardently desired, you fool of fame," I cry out and a mighty irony takes hold of me.

And then I stretch out my legs until my feet reach the end of the coffin, nestle my head amid the flowers, and make ready to enjoy my great peace with all my might. I am not in the least frightened or confounded, for I know that air to breathe will never again be lacking now for I need it no longer. I am dead, properly and honestly dead. Nothing remains now but to flow peacefully and gently into the realm of the unconscious, and to let the dim dream of the All surge over me to eternity.

"Good-night, my dear former fellow-creatures," I say and turn contemptuously on my other side. "You can all go to the dickens for all I care."

And then I determine to lie still as a mouse and discover whether I cannot find some food for the malice that yet is in me, by listening to man's doings upon the wretched earth above me.

At first I hear nothing but a dull roaring. But that may proceed as well from the subterranean waters that rush through the earth somewhere in my neighbourhood. But no, the sound comes from above. And from time to time I also hear a rattling and hissing as of dried peas poured out over a sieve.

"Of course, it's wretched weather again," I say and rub my hands comfortably, not, to be sure, without knocking my elbows against the side of the coffin.

"They could have made this place a little roomier," I say to myself. But when it occurs to me that, in my character of an honest corpse,

I have no business to move at all if I want to be a credit to my new station.

But the spirit of contradiction in me at once rebels against this imputation.

"There are no classes in the grave and no prejudices," I cry. "In the grave we are all alike, high and low, poor and rich. The rags of the beggar, my masters, have here just the same value as the purple cloak that falls from the shoulders of a king. Here even the laurel loses its significance as the crown of fame and is given to many a one."

I cease, for my fingers have discovered a riband that hangs from the wreath. Upon it, I am justified in assuming, there is written some flattering legend. The letters are just raised enough to be indistinctly felt.

I am about to call for matches, but remember just in time that it is forbidden to strike a light in the grave or rather, that it is contrary to the very conception of the grave to be illuminated.

This thought annoys me and I continue: "The laurel is given here not to the distinguished alone. I must correct that expression. Are not we corpses distinguished *per se* as compared to the miserable plebeian living? Is not this noble rest in which we dwell an unmistakable sign of true aristocracy? And the laurel that is given to the dead, that laurel, my masters, fills me with as high a pride as would the diadem of a king."

I ceased. For I could rightly expect enthusiastic applause at the close of this effective passage. But as everything remained silent I turned my thoughts once more upon myself, and considered, too, that my finest speeches would find no public here.

"It is, besides, in utter contradiction to the conception of death to deliver speeches," I said to myself, but at once I began another in order to establish an opposition against myself.

"Conception? What is a conception? What do I care for conceptions here? I am dead. I have earned the sacred right to disregard such things. If those two-penny living creatures cannot imagine the grave otherwise than dark or the dead otherwise than dumb—why, I surely have no need to care for that."

In the meantime my fingers had scratched about on the riband in the vain hope of inferring from the gilt and raised letters on the silk their form and perhaps the significance of the legend. My efforts were, however, without success. Hence I continued outraged: "In order to speak first of the conception of the grave as dark, I should like to ask any intelligent and expert corpse: 'Why is the grave necessarily dark?' Should not we who are dead rather demand of

an age that has made such enormous progress
in illumination, which has not only invented gas
and electric lighting and complied with the regu-
lations for the illumination of streets, but has at
a slight cost succeeded in giving to every corner
of the world the very light of day—may we not
demand of such an age that it put an end to the
old-fashioned darkness of the grave? It would
seem as if the most elementary piety would con-
strain the living to this improvement. But when
did the living ever feel any piety? We must
enforce from them the necessaries of a worthy
existence in death. Gentlemen, I close with the
last, or, I had better say, the first words of our
great Goethe whose genius with characteristic
power of divination foresaw the unworthy condition of the inner grave and the necessities of
a truly noble and liberal minded corpse. For
what else could be the meaning of that saying
which I herewith inscribe upon our banner:
'Light, more light!' That must henceforth be
our device and our battlecry."

This time, too, silence was my only answer.
Whence I inferred that in the grave there is
neither striving nor crying out. Nevertheless I
continued to amuse myself and made many a
speech against the management of the cemetery,
against the insufficiency of the method of flat
pressure upon the dead now in use, and similar

outrages. In the meantime the storm above had
raged and the rain lashed its fill and a peaceful
silence descended upon all things.

Only from time to time did I hear a short, dull
uniform thunder, which I could not account for
until it occurred to me that it was produced by
the footsteps of passers-by, the noise of which
was thus echoed and multiplied in the earth.

And then suddenly I heard the sound of
human voices.

The sound came vertically down to my head.

People seemed to be standing at my grave.

"Much I care about you," I said, and was
about to continue to reflect on my epoch-making invention which is to be called: *'Helminothanatos,'* that is to say, 'Death by Worms' and
which, so soon as it is completed is to be registered in the patent office as number 156,763.
But my desire to know what was thought of me
after my death left me no rest. Hence I did
not hesitate long to press my ear to the inner
roof of the coffin in order that the sound might
better reach me thus.

Now I recognised the voices at once.

They belonged to two men to whom I had
always been united by bonds of the tenderest
sympathy and whom I was proud to call my
friends. They had always assured me of the high
value which they set upon me and that their

blame—with which they had often driven me to
secret despair—proceeded wholly from helpful
and unselfish love.

"Poor devil," one of them said, in a tone of
such humiliating compassion that I was ashamed
of myself in the very grave.

"He had to bite the dust pretty early," the
other sighed. "But it was better so both for
him and for myself. I could not have held him
above water much longer." . . .

From sheer astonishment I knocked my head
so hard against the side of the coffin that a bump
remained.

"When did you ever hold me above water?"
I wanted to cry out but I considered that they
could not hear me.

Then the first one spoke again.

"I often found it hard enough to aid him
with my counsel without wounding his vanity.
For we know how vain he was and how taken
with himself."

"And yet he achieved little enough," the other
answered. "He ran after women and sought the
society of inferior persons for the sake of their
flattery. It always astonished me anew when
he managed to produce something of approxi-
mately solid worth. For neither his character
nor his intelligence gave promise of it."

"In your wonderful charity you are capable

of finding something excellent even in his work," the other replied. "But let us be frank: The only thing he sometimes succeeded in doing was to flatter the crude instincts of the mob. True earnestness or conviction he never possessed."

"I never claimed either for him," the first eagerly broke in. "Only I didn't want to deny the poor fellow that bit of piety which is demanded. *De mortuis*——"

And both voices withdraw into the distance.

"O you grave-robbers!" I cried and shook my fist after them. "Now I know what your friendship was worth. Now it is clear to me how you humiliated me upon all my ways, and how when I came to you in hours of depression you administered a kick in order that you might increase in stature at my expense! Oh, if I could only." . . .

I ceased laughing.

"What silly wishes, old boy!" I admonished myself. "Even if you could master your friends; your enemies would drive you into the grave a thousand times over."

And I determined to devote my whole thought henceforth to the epoch-making invention of my impregnating fluid called *"Helminothanatos"* or "Death by Worms."

But new voices roused me from my meditation.

I LISTENED.

"That's where what's his name is buried," said one.

"Quite right," said the other. "I gave him many a good hit while he was among us—more than I care to think about to-day. But he was an able fellow. His worst enemy couldn't deny that."

I started and shuddered.

I knew well who he was: my bitterest opponent who tortured me so long with open lashes and hidden stabs that I almost ended by thinking I deserved nothing else.

And he had a good word to say for me— *he?*

His voice went on. "To-day that he is out of our way we may as well confess that we always liked him a great deal. He took life and work seriously and never used an indecent weapon against us. And if the tactics of war had not forced us to represent his excellences as faults, we might have learned a good deal from him."

"It's a great pity," said the other. "If, before everything was at sixes and sevens, he could have been persuaded to adopt our views, we could perhaps have had the pleasure of receiving him into our fighting lines."

"With open arms," was the answer. And
then in solemn tone:

"Peace be to his ashes."

The other echoed: "Peace . . ."

And then they went on. . . .

I hid my face in my hands. My breast seemed
to expand and gently, very gently something
began to beat in it which had rested in silent
numbness since I lay down here.

"So that is the nature of the world's judgment," I said to myself. "I should have known
that before. With head proudly erect I would
have gone my way, uninfluenced by the glitter of
false affection as by the blindness of wildly aiming hatred. I would have shaken praise and
blame from me with the same joyous laugh and
sought the norm of achievement in myself alone.
Oh, if only I could live once more! If only
there were a way out of these accursed six
boards!"

In impotent rage I pounded the coffin top
with my fist and only succeeded in running a
splinter into my finger.

And then there came over me once more, even
though it came hesitatingly and against my will,
a delightful consciousness of that eternal peace
into which I had entered.

"Would it be worth the trouble after all," I
said to myself, "to return to the fray once more,

even if I were a thousand times certain of victory? What is this victory worth? Even if I succeed in being the first to mount some height untrod hitherto by any human foot, yet the next generation will climb on my shoulders and hurl me down into the abysm of oblivion. There I could lie, lonely and helpless, until the six boards are needed again to help me to my happiness. And so let me be content and wait until that thing in my breast which has began to beat so impudently, has become quiet once more."

I stretched myself out, folded my hands, and determined to hold no more incendiary speeches and thus counteract the trade of the worms, but rather to doze quietly into the All.

Thus I lay again for a space.

Then arose somewhere a strange musical sound, which penetrated my dreamy state but partially at first before it awakened me wholly from my slumber.

What was that? A signal of the last day?

"It's all the same to me," I said and stretched myself. "Whether it's heaven or hell—it will be a new experience."

But the sound that had awakened me had nothing in common with the metallic blare of trumpets which religious guides have taught us to expect.

Gentle and insinuating, now like the tones of

flutes played by children, now like the sobbing
of a girl's voice, now like the caressing sweetness with which a mother speaks to her little child
—so infinitely manifold but always full of sweet
and yearning magic—alien and yet dear and familiar—such was the music that came to my
ear.

"Where have I heard that before?" I asked
myself, listening.

And as I thought and thought, an evening of
spring arose before my soul—an evening out of
a far and perished time. . . . I had wandered along the bank of a steaming river. The
sunset which shone through the jagged young
leaves spread a purple carpet over the quiet
waters upon which only a swift insect would here
and there create circular eddies. At every step
I took the dew sprang up before me in gleaming pearls, and a fragrance of wild thyme and
roses floated through the air. . . .

There it must have been that I heard this
music for the first time.

And now it was all clear: The nightingale was
singing . . . the nightingale.

And so spring has come to the upper world.

Perhaps it is an evening of May even as that
which my spirit recalls.

Blue flowers stand upon the meadows. . . .
Goldenrod and lilac mix their blossoms into gold

and violet wreaths. . . . Like torn veils the delicate flakings of the buttercups fly through the twilight. . . .

Surely from the village sounds the stork's rattle . . . and surely the distant strains of an accordion are heard. . . .

But the nightingale up there cares little what other music may be made. It sobs and jubilates louder and louder, as if it knew that in the poor dead man's bosom down here the heart beats once more stormily against his side.

And at every throb of that heart a hot stream glides through my veins. It penetrates farther and farther until it will have filled my whole body. It seems to me as though I must cry out with yearning and remorse. But my dull stubbornness arises once more: "You have what you desired. So lie here and be still, even though you should be condemned to hear the nightingale's song until the end of the world.

The song has grown much softer.

Obviously the human steps that now encircle my grave with their sullen resonance have driven the bird to a more distant bush.

"Who may it be," I ask myself, "that thinks of wandering to my place of rest on an evening of May when the nightingales are singing."

And I listen anew.

It sounds almost as though some one up there were weeping.

Did I not go my earthly road lonely and unloved? Did I not die in the house of a stranger? Was I not huddled away in the earth by strangers? Who is it that comes to weep at my grave?

And each one of the tears that is shed above there falls glowing upon my breast. . . .

And my breast rises in a convulsive struggle but the coffin lid pushes it back. I strain my head against the wood to burst it, but it lies upon me like a mountain. My body seems to burn. To protect it I burrow in the saw-dust which fills mouth and eyes with its biting chaff.

I try to cry out but my throat is paralysed.

I want to pray but instead of thoughts the lightnings of madness shoot through my brain.

I feel only one thing that threatens to dissolve all my body into a stream of flame and that penetrates my whole being with immeasurable might: "I must live . . . live . . .!"

There, in my sorest need, I think of the faery who upon my desire brought me by magic to my grave.

"Thea, I beseech you. I have sinned against the world and myself. It was cowardly and slothful to doubt of life so long as a spark of life and power glowed in my veins. Let me arise,

I beseech you, from the torments of hell—let me arise!"

And behold: the boards of the coffin fall from me like a wornout garment. The earth rolls down on both sides of me and unites beneath me in order to raise my body.

I open my eyes and perceive myself to be lying in dark grass. Through the bent limbs of trees the grave stars look down upon me. The black crosses stand in the evening glow, and past the railings of grave-plots my eyes blink out into the blossoming world.

The crickets chirp about me in the grass, and the nightingale begins to sing anew.

Half dazed I pull myself together.

Waves of fragrance and melting shadows extend into the distance.

Suddenly I see next to me on the grave mound a crouching gray figure. Between a veil tossed back I see a countenance, pallid and lovely, with smooth dark hair and a madonna-like face. About the softly smiling mouth is an expression of gentle loftiness such as is seen in those martyrs who joyfully bleed to death from the mightiness of their love.

Her eyes look down upon me in smiling peace, clear and soulful, the measure of all goodness, the mirror of all beauty.

I know the dark gleam of those eyes, I know

that gray, soft veil, I know that poor sick hand, white as a blossom, that leans upon a crutch.

It is she, my faery, whose tears have awakened me from the dead.

All my defiance vanishes.

I lie upon the earth before her and kiss the hem of her garment.

And she inclines her head and stretches her hand out to me.

With the help of that hand I arise.

Holding this poor, sick hand, I stride joyfully back into life.

VI.

I sought my faery and I found her not.

I sought her upon the flowery fields of the South and on the ragged moors of the Northland; in the eternal snow of Alpine ridges and in the black folds of the nether earth; in the iridescent glitter of the boulevard and in the sounding desolation of the sea. . . . And I found her not.

I sought her amid the tobacco smoke and the cheap applause of popular assemblies and on the vanity fair of the professional social patron; in the brilliance of glittering feasts I sought her and in the twilit silence of domestic comfort. . . . And I found her not.

My eye thirsted for the sight of her but in my memory there was no mark by which I could have recognised her. Each image of her was confused and obliterated by the screaming colours of a new epoch.

Good and evil in a thousand shapes had come between me and my faery. And the evil had grown into good for me, the good into evil.

But the sum of evil was greater than the sum

of good. I bent low under the burden, and for a long space my eyes saw nothing but the ground to which I clung.

And therefore did I need my faery.

I needed her as a slave needs liberation, as the master needs a higher master, as the man of faith needs heaven.

In her I sought my resurrection, my strength to live, my defiant illusion.

And therefore was I famished for her.

My ear listened to all the confusing noises that were about me, but the voice of my faery was not among them. My hand groped after alien hands, but the faery hand was not among them. Nor would I have recognised it.

And then I went in quest of her to all the ends of the earth.

First I went to a philosopher.

"You know everything, wise man," I said, "can you tell me how I may find my faery again?"

The philosopher put the tips of his five outstretched fingers against his vaulted forehead and, having meditated a while, said: "You must seek, through pure intuition, to grasp all the conceptual essence of the being of the object sought for. Therefore withdraw into yourself and listen to the voice of your mind."

I did as I was told. But the rushing of the blood in the shells of my ears affrighted me. It drowned every other voice.

Next I went to a very clever physician and asked him the same question.

The physician who was about to invent an artifically digested porridge in order to save the modern stomach any exertion, let his spoon fall for a moment and said: "You must take only such foods as will tend to add phosphorous matter to the brain. The answer to your question will then come of itself."

I followed his directions but instead of my faery a number of confusing images presented themselves. I saw in the hearts of those who were about me faery gardens and infernos, deserts and turnip fields; I saw a comically hopping rainworm who was nibbling at a graceful centipede; I saw a world in which darkness was lord. I saw much else and was frightened at the images.

Then I went to a clergyman and put my question to him.

The pious man comfortably lit his pipe and said: "You will find no faeries mentioned in the catechism, my friend. Hence there are none, and it is sin to seek them. But perhaps you can help me bring back the devil into the world, the old, authentic devil with tail and horns and sulphurous stench. He really exists and we need him."

After I had made inquiry of a learned jurist who advised me to have my faery located by the police, I went to one of my colleagues, a poet of the classic school.

I found him clad in a red silk dressing gown, a wet handkerchief tied around his forehead. Its purpose was to keep his all too stormy wealth of inspiration in check. Before him on the table stood a glassful of Malaga wine and a silver salver full of pomegranates and grapes. The grapes were made of glass and the pomegranates of soap. But the contemplation of them was meant to heighten his mood. Near him, nailed to the floor, stood a golden harp on which was hung a laurel wreath and a nightcap.

Timidly I put my question and the honoured master spoke: "The muse, my worthy friend— ask the muse. Ask the muse who leads us poor children of the dust into the divine sanctuary; carried aloft by whose wings into the heights of ether we feel truly human—ask her!"

As it would have been necessary for me, first of all, to look up this unknown lady, I went to another colleague—one of the modern seekers of truth.

I found him at his desk peering through a microscope at a dying flee which he was studying carefully. He noted each of its movements upon the slips of paper from which he later constructed his works. Next to him stood some bread and cheese, a little bottle full of ether and a box of powders.

When I had explained my business he grew very angry.

"Man, don't bother me with such rot!" he cried. "Faeries and elves and ideas and the devil knows what—that's all played out. That's worse than iambics. Go hang, you idiot, and don't disturb me."

Sad at seeing myself and my faery so contemned, I crept away and went to one of those modern artists in life, who had tasted with epicurean fineness all the esctasies and sorrows of earthly life in order to broaden his personality. . . . I hoped that he would understand me, too.

I found him lying on a *chaise longue,* smoking a cigarette, and turning the leaves of a French novel. It was *Là-bas* by Huysmans, and he didn't even cut the leaves, being too lazy.

He heard my question with an obliging smile. "Dear friend, let's be honest. The thing is simple. A faery is a woman. That is certain. Well, take up with every woman that runs into your arms. Love them all—one after another.

You'll be sure then to hit upon your faery some day."

As I feared that to follow this advice I would have to waste the better part of my life and all my conscience, I chose a last and desperate method and went to a magician.

If Manfred had forced Astarte back into being, though only for a fleeting moment, why could I not do the same with the dear ruler of my higher will?

I found a dignified man with the eyes of an enthusiast and filthy locks. He was badly in need of a change of linen. And so I had every reason to consider him an idealist.

He talked a good real of "Karma," of "materialisations" and of the "plurality of spheres." He used many other strange words by means of which he made it clear to me that my faery would reveal herself to me only by his help.

With beating heart I entered a dark room at the appointed hour. The magician led me in.

A soft, mysterious music floated toward me. I was left alone, pressed to the door, awaiting the things that were to come in breathless fear.

Suddenly, as I was waiting in the darkness, a gleaming, bluish needle protruded from the floor. It grew to rings and became a snake which breathed forth flames and dissolved into flame. . . .

And the tongues of these flames played on all sides and finally parted in curves like the leaves of an opening lotos flower, out of whose calix white veils arose slowly, very slowly, and became as they glided upward the garments of a woman who looked at me, who was lashed by fear, with sightless eyes.

"Are you Thea?" I asked trembling.

The veils inclined in affirmation.

"Where do you dwell?"

The veils waved, shaken by the trembling limbs.

"Ask me after other things," a muffled voice said.

"Why do you no longer appear to me?"

"I may not."

"Who hinders you?"

"You." . . .

"By what? Am I unworthy of you?"

"Yes."

In deep contrition I was about to fall at her feet. But, coming nearer, I perceived that my faery's breath smelled of onions.

This circumstance sobered me a bit, for I don't like onions.

I knocked at the locked door, paid my magician what I owed him and went my way.

From now on all hope of ever seeing her again vanished. But my soul cried out after her.

And the world receded from me. Its figures dislimned into things that have been, its noise did not thunder at my threshold. A solitariness half voluntary and half enforced dragged its steps through my house. Only a few, the intimates of my heart and brothers of my blood, surrounded my life with peace and kept watch without my doors.

It was a late afternoon near Advent Sunday.

But no message of Christmas came to my yearning soul.

Somewhere, like a discarded toy, lay amid rubbish the motive power of my passions. My heart was dumb, my hand nerveless, and even need—that last incentive—had slackened to a wild memory.

The world was white with frost. . . . The dust of ice and the rain of star-light filled the world . . . cloths of glittering white covered the plains. . . . The bare twigs of the trees stretched upwards like staves of coral. . . . The fir trees trembled like spun glass.

A red sunset spread its reflection over all. But the sunset itself was poverty stricken. No purple lights, no gleam of seven colours warmed the whiteness of the world. Not like the gentle farewell of the sun but cruel as the threat of

paralysing night did the bloody stripe stare
through my window.

It is the hour of afternoon tea. The regula-
tions of the house demand that.

Grayish blue steam whirls up to the shadowed
ceiling and moistens with falling drops the
rounded silver of the tea urn.

The bell rings.

From the housekeeper's rooms floats an odour
of fresh baked breads. They are having a feast
there. Perhaps they mean to prepare one for
the master, too.

A new book that has come a great distance to-
day is in my hand.

I read. Another one has made the great discovery that the world begins with him.

Ah, did it not once begin with me, too?

To be young, to be young! Ah, even if one
suffers need—only to be young!

But who, after all, would care to retrace the
difficult road?

Perhaps you, O woman at my side?

I would wager that even you would not.

And I raise a questioning glance though I
know her to be far . . . and who stands behind the kettle, framed by the rising of the bluish
steam?

Ah child, have I not seen you often—you with
the brownish locks and the dark lashes over blue

eyes . . . you with the bird-like twitter in the throbbing whiteness of your throat, and the light-hearted step?

And yet, did I ever see you? Did I ever see that look which surrounds me with its ripe wisdom and guesses the secrets of my heart? Did I ever see that mouth so rich and firm at once which smiles upon me full of reticent consolation and alluring comprehension?

Who are you, child, that you dare to look me through and through, as though I had laid my confidence at your feet? Who are you that you dare to descend wingless into the abysms of my soul, that you can smile away my torture and my suffocation?

Why did you not come earlier in your authentic form? Why did you not come as all that which you are to me and will be from this hour on?

Why do you hide yourself in the mist which renders my recognition turbid and shadows your outlines?

Come to me, for you are she whom I seek, for whom my heart's blood yearns in order to flow as sacrifice and triumph!

You are the faery who clarifies my eye and steels my will, who brings to me upon her young hands my own youth!

Come to me and do not leave me again as you have so often left me!

I start up to stretch out my arms to her and see how her glance becomes estranged and her smile as of stone. As one who is asleep with open eyes, thus she stands there and stares past me.

I try to find her, to clasp her, to force her spirit to see me. Without repulsing me she glides softly from me. . . . The walls open. . . . The stones of the stairs break. . . . We flee out into the wintry silence. . . .

She glides before me over the pallid velvet of the road . . . over the tinkling glass of the frozen heath . . . through the glittering boughs. She smiles—for whom?

The hilly fields, hardened by the frost, the bushes scattering ice—everything obstructs my way. I break through and follow her.

But she glides on before me, scarcely a foot above the ground, but farther, farther . . . over the broken earth, down the precipice . . . to the lake whose bluish surface of new ice melts in the distance into the afterglow.

Now she hangs over the bank like a cloud of smoke, and the wind that blows upon my back, raises the edges of her dress like triangular pennants.

"Stay, Thea. . . . I cannot follow you across the lake! . . . The water will not up-bear a mortal." . . .

But the rising wind pushes her irresistibly on. . . .

Now I stand as the edge of the lake. The thin ice forces upward great hollow bubbles. . . .

Will it suffer my groping feet? Will it break and whelm me in brackish water and morass?

There is no room for hesitation. For already the wind is sweeping her afar.

And I venture out upon the glassy floor which is no floor at all, but which a brief frost threw as a deceptive mirror across the deep.

It bears me up for five paces, for six, for ten. Then suddenly the cry of harps is in my ear and something like an earthquake quivers through my limbs. And this sound grows into a mighty crunching and waxes into thunder which sounds afar and returns from the distance in echoing detonation.

But at my left hand glitters a cleft which furrows the ice with manicoloured splinters and runs from me into the invisible.

What is to be done? On . . . on . . .!

And again the harps cry out and a great rattling flies forth and returns as thunder. And again a great cleft opens its brilliant hues at my side.

On, on . . . to seek her smiling, even though the smile is not for me. It will be for me if only I can grasp the hem of her garment.

A third cleft opens; a fourth crosses it, uniting it to the first.

I must cross. But I dare not jump, for the ice must not crumble lest an abysm open at my feet.

It is no longer a sheet of ice upon which I travel—it is a net-work of clefts. Between them lies something blue and all but invisible that bears me by the merest chance. I can see the tangled water grasses wind about and the polished fishes dart whom my body will feed unless a miracle happens.

Lit by the gathering afterglow a plain of fire stretches out before me, and far on the horizon the saving shore looms dark.

Farther . . . farther!

Sinister and deceptive springs arise to my right and left and hurl their waters across my path. . . . A soft gurgling is heard and at last drowns the resonant sound of thunder.

Farther, farther. . . . Mere life is at stake.

There in the distance a cloud dislimns which but now lured me to death with its girlish smile. What do I care now?

The struggle endures for eternities.

The wind drives me on. I avoid the clefts,
wade through the springs; I measure the distances, for now I have to jump. . . . The
depths are yawning about me.

The ice under my feet begins to rock. It
rocks like a cradle, heaving and falling at every
step. . . . It would be a charming game
were it not a game with death

My breath comes flying . . . my heart-
beats throttle me . . . sparks quiver before
my eyes.

Let me rock . . . rock . . . rock
back to the dark sources of being.

A springing fountain, higher than all the
others, hisses up before me. . . . Edges and
clods rise into points. . . .

One spring . . . the last of all . . .
hopeless . . . inspired by the desperate will
to live. . . .

Ah, what is that?

Is that not the goodly earth beneath my feet
—the black, hard, stable earth?

It is but a tiny islet formed of frozen mud
and roots; it is scarcely two paces across, but
large enough to give security to my sinking
body.

I am ashore, saved, for only a few arm lengths
from me arises the reedy line of the shore.

A drove of wild ducks rises in diagonal flight.

. . . Purple radiance pours through the twigs of trees. . . . From nocturnal heavens the first stars shine upon me.

The ghostly game is over! The faery hunt is as an end.

One truth I realise: He who has firm ground under his feet needs no faeries.

And serenely I stride into the sunset world.